Show Me a Marriage of Convenience

Cowboy Crossing
~ Book 1 ~

D1713996

By

ALEXA VERDE

Cover Art by Julia Gussman
Edited by Deidre Lockhart.

ISBN: 9798698816669

An ex-player cowboy with a little son, the boy's shy plus-size aunt, and a reluctant modern marriage of convenience only the boy is excited about… A sweet, clean, wholesome romance with a happily-ever-after!

After three near-death experiences in one day—okay, maybe burning dinner and falling from a tree shouldn't count—Kade Clark worries about his son's future if he's not around to protect him. The last thing he wants is for his son to become a bargaining chip between a con artist grandfather and a ruthless ex trying to get their hands on the family fortune. So Kade agrees to a crazy proposal from the woman his child adores. But as a former foster kid, Kade learned to walk away before getting hurt. Can he now learn to stay and love?

Heather Johnson dreams of a real marriage with the man her sister abandoned, not a fake one. But the rumor is Kade might leave their small town again and take her darling nephew with him. She's reluctant to trust a womanizer—husband or not. If she allows love for him to ignite her heart, will her marshmallow-soft heart become roasted and burned?

To Trudy ~

To Trudy, whose friendship and encouragement I treasure very much.

CHAPTER ONE

"WILL YOU MARRY ME?" Heather Johnson blurted out.

"Excuse me?"

As Kade Clark's square jaw slackened and he coughed and spluttered, Heather scooted back a step to avoid his spilling coffee. Then she tried to keep her chin up when he stared at her as if she'd hit him with her skillet instead of asking him to marry her.

Unfortunately, she'd chosen to ask when he'd slugged back the black coffee she'd made. His adorable little boy of not-quite-five—her darling nephew—giggled as he shoved the rest of the waffle he'd requested for breakfast into his mouth.

"Daddy made a mess. Daddy made a mess," Landon sing-songed.

The child probably felt vindicated because he was usually the one making messes at meals. Kade wiped the spill with a napkin while Heather tightened her grip on the skillet to keep herself anchored in the kitchen.

Well, as shocked as Kade must be, he couldn't be in worse shape than she was. She twisted her grip on the skillet, wishing she could take back the words and just continue being Landon's babysitter, despite her promise to her father.

Heat, having nothing to do with the stove, roiled her. Seriously, *how* had she just said that? She dropped rather than placed the skillet on the stove, then turned the stove off, only vaguely noticing Kade pouring himself another cup of coffee.

The kid was eating. That's what mattered. The breakfast for adults should wait, or she'd burn something—ahem, something more than the bridges she was burning behind herself.

In her dreams as a teen, the proposal involved a handsome man—the love of her life—on his bended knee, a sparkling diamond ring, an equally sparkling dress decorated with a diamond necklace, a fancy dinner, preferably in Paris, and a few fireworks.

Instead, at forty, she was proposing to the man she loved to hate, in his kitchen, before making a fancy meal of fried eggs and bacon.

Never mind that she was wearing baggy jeans to hide all those pesky extra pounds and a white T-shirt a size too big, decorated with a lard stain, and the only things sparkling were the glamorous drops of sweat bejeweling her forehead.

Marvelous.

She swallowed hard.

"*You* want to be married to *me?*" His enticing dark eyes widened.

Maybe she shouldn't call his eyes enticing. But when he as much as looked at her, her insides turned into mush.

Like now.

Nonsense.

No reason for it.

She'd known him since she'd been a teen, watched from afar as the infamous boy from one of the richest families in town had dated a different girl nearly every week. After finishing high school and working at the family ranch, he'd worked at oil rigs in Texas, then as a foreman at a cattle ranch in Montana, then at an equestrian ranch in Kentucky.

Then, after a summer at home before his thirty-third birthday, he married her sister. Everyone agreed they'd been the most beautiful couple Cowboy Crossing had ever seen.

Kade joined the family business helping his older brother manage Mending Hearts Ranch in their beloved Missouri. Then the beautiful couple had a baby boy nine months later.

Heather had ended up babysitting her nephew since her gorgeous sister couldn't be bothered with such trifles. At least, she'd babysat him until the family moved to California for her sister's acting career.

Later, when Kade, sulking and wifeless, returned with his son, Heather started helping him full time. He'd probably gotten so used to her he considered her something like furniture.

Today, that furniture was talking.

"Nooo." She shook her head for emphasis and leaned against the counter, resisting the urge to crank up the air conditioner. "I don't want to be married to you. I'd rather walk on hot coals than be married to you."

Okay, maybe that was an exaggeration, but her face was flaming up as if she held hot coals close to it.

"Phew. That's a relief." He laughed as if he didn't hear the last sentence. "Lack of sleep must be playing a trick on my—"

Landon let out a squeal as their dog, Dara, a big five-year-old part-Newfoundland, ran into the room. So Heather didn't hear the rest of the sentence.

"Stay!" Kade and Heather said to the dog, and she dropped on the tiled floor.

"I wasn't gonna go anywhere." Confusion clouded the boy's eyes.

"We meant the dog." Heather refilled his orange juice glass and couldn't resist placing a quick kiss atop his head.

As tenderness filled her, her insides turned to mush for a totally different reason.

For this little boy, she'd have to finish the conversation. As well as for her promise to her father, who'd believed the rumors Kade intended to leave for Montana again. He'd had a great job offer at a ranch where he'd worked before. Back when he'd been a wanderer, an adventurer even.

That meant, they'd lose Landon. Neither her father nor she could bear the thought of it.

"Dara, Daddy's gonna marry Auntie H!" the boy announced to the dog and clapped.

The pet barked cheerfully as if giving her approval.

Kade groaned. "No. This is just some big misunderstanding."

"Oh. That's too bad." Landon sighed, then drained his orange juice and thudded his glass on the table. "I'm gonna go play with the dog."

Dara perked up and rose to her paws, giving out a cheerful bark.

Her mind whirling, Heather walked the child into the spacious living room.

Kade had bought this house together with the adjacent cattle ranch when he'd come back from California—a house so different from the one he'd bought for her sister with expensive furniture ordered online and jaw-dropping pricey art.

That house had suited Josephine, though. The place had been like somebody in gorgeous clothes and expensive makeup, but whose smile never reached their eyes.

This place, with exposed brick, a fireplace that often greeted them with fire, simple but steady furniture, piles of toys everywhere, and Landon's drawings taped to the walls, seemed ready to give you a friendly hug. Just like the large plush puppy in the living room corner sitting on his behind and holding his front paws wide open for an embrace.

"I don't want to be married to you," she repeated as she returned to the breakfast nook overlooking a green lawn. "But I think it's for the best for all three of us. Really. Look, we can sign a prenup. Name your conditions. I don't care. I just want to be there for Landon." She talked fast so she couldn't change her mind and stop herself.

She'd agreed to her father's request because she'd been sure Kade would say no right off.

Right?

Why was she trying to persuade him then?

"You *are* serious." His jaw slackened for the second time as he cradled his new cup of coffee.

Taking a deep breath of coffee-scented air, she gathered her courage from where it tried to slither into the tiled floor. Her pulse rushing in her ears drowned any lucid thinking.

There was a tiny crack in one of the tiles. Suddenly, it bothered her as if it were an exposed vein. Like her heart being currently exposed. And maybe she used to have a crush—tiny!—on Kade as a teen, but she'd known better than to let herself grow feelings for a player.

"I know it sounds ridiculous right now, but... Just think about it."

This little boy was worth making herself look stupid.

She fisted her hands at her sides and met Kade's gaze.

The guy shook his head. "I don't need to think about it."

Her heart sank.

But then, what did she count on?

Bad enough that he was two years her junior, did he also have to resemble that guy from the spicy cologne commercial? Right down to the rugged looks, the broad shoulders, the tight T-shirt showcasing muscles enhanced by manual outdoor labor. Plus that twinkle in the eye. Charisma still oozed from him like it had when he'd been eighteen and turned even the grown women's heads in their small town.

Or... He wouldn't think she was a gold digger, would he?

"It's not about your money," she added. "I make enough from my IT business, doing web design and software development. I just want to be close to Landon. And you know he needs a mother figure."

Leaning back in his chair, Kade frowned, the expression of his dark eyes hooded. "Why would I want to get married again? I already had one disastrous marriage. And no offense, but you're not my type. Except when you're with my son, you're always so stern and... stuck up."

Stuck up?

Her?

The guy couldn't be serious. Didn't he know her *at all*?

She'd been in his life, in his house, for years after all. And maybe she had a problem with self-esteem—okay, so she *definitely* had a self-esteem problem—but it went waaaay in the other direction.

She tipped her chin as she pulled up her glasses, her indignation rising. "I'm not stern or stuck up."

"You told me I knew no difference between *they're* and *their* and scolded me for my dirty boots."

Her chin went even higher. "Well, you do mix those words, and your boots were dirty a few days ago."

"I appreciate you helping me with Landon, I really do." His shaking head contradicted his words. "Especially after those three nannies bailed out on me when you took a vacation. What's wrong with keeping things the way they are? We don't like each other much, but we tolerate each other for the sake of the child."

Huh.

"Sounds like a lot of marriages." Had she said that aloud?

What was wrong with her today?

Still, she'd seen it growing up all too well. Well, her father had loved her mother enough to work two jobs to please her, but it had always gone unappreciated.

Then there was that... issue. Something about Kade had always drawn her to him, probably the reason she'd been harsh with him from time to time to hide her silly attraction.

She stifled a snort.

Her and likely the entire female population of Cowboy Crossing had been drawn to him! Not to mention the little detail that he'd dated and shotgun married her older sister, for crying out loud.

In her family, she'd always been the sensible one. She wouldn't fall for the town's most famous cowboy player.

Even if she had a healthy dose of respect for how he'd turned his life around since his troubled youthful years. For how he'd become a ranch owner almost as good as his older brother—and that was saying something—and added more cattle ranches, bigger hay production, and a sizable equestrian ranch where they raised Thoroughbreds, some of which placed in or won races.

His conversations with his employees and family members showcased how much he'd wised up, grown to care not just about his son but also about his employees and the family business he'd initially wanted nothing to do with.

Deep inside, she'd supported his dream of adding an equestrian ranch for foster kids like him. But other than sharing difficult childhoods and teen years, they were opposites in every way. Her proposal didn't make sense.

She wouldn't even be here, in his kitchen every day making meals and helping out if it wasn't for her nephew. Now, her love for the two most important men in her life—no, not Kade, but her father and her nephew—had made her agree to Dad's crazy, crazy, crazy—did she mention crazy?—idea.

Those rumors might be true. Kade might up and leave and take the kid with him.

So she'd take drastic measures. As a wife, even if in name only, she'd have some say in her precious nephew's well-being.

He studied her, those chiseled features smoothing out somewhat. "Besides, what if you meet some guy and fall in love with him?"

Something flashed in his eyes. Jealousy or wishful thinking? And why did she desperately want to know?

"When you're already married to me, fake marriage or not, from what I know about you, you wouldn't cheat." That emotion she couldn't quite name lingered in his gaze.

When he looked at her like that, it gave her goosebumps, but... in a pleasant way. Her father's idea about her marrying Kade sounded more and more ridiculous. Then her gaze fell on a puppy drawing taped to the wall.

Of course, Kade wouldn't accept her idea. She didn't have her sister's gorgeous looks or bright personality or melodic laughter or slim body or... She should stop there. After many of the guys who'd dated her had switched to dating her sister, Heather had accepted it. But she did have a brain that allowed her to work in IT from home and make a decent salary, and she had a heart full of love for her nephew.

She thrust her hands onto her hips. "I already have a guy who I adore and who has my whole heart."

Again, something unreadable flashed in his eyes. "What about him? Does he love you back?"

As Landon giggled in the living room, her heart melted. "I think he does."

A muscle moved in his jaw. "Then why would you want to be married to *me*?"

"I'm talking about Landon!" She laughed, and the kid laughed as if he were in on the joke.

She had no issues foregoing the romance that hadn't existed in her life these last years. Since her fiancé's betrayal, she hadn't trusted men, and since she'd gained more and more weight comfort eating, they hadn't exactly been chasing after her.

Kade, however, had it the other way around.

She leaned forward slightly. "Think about it. I'll be here taking care of Landon full time. You'd even be able to have a buddy's night with your friends again. Finally take a vacation. You won't have to call me and feel guilty when you want to see your family or work late."

He lifted his arms in a mocking surrender. "I do love my son, you know. I love spending time with him."

Hope unraveled inside her. That was what she was counting on.

Just breathe in the coffee's aroma. Do not notice his spicy cologne mingling with it.

"I know." She poured herself a cup of coffee and added a generous helping of cream but didn't lift it, too nervous to drink.

He took a sip of his coffee, obviously chilled about the whole situation while she was trembling inside. "But what about me? What about my freedom? What if I meet someone else and fall in love with her?"

Jealousy cut razor-sharp.

Right.

Like she had a right to be jealous. "From what I heard, you already dated nearly every attractive single female of your age in Cowboy Crossing and the few towns around. Unless you want to expand your pool by age or geography, spending some time without dating shouldn't be that hard."

She should know. She'd forgone dating for years.

"How long?" One of his smooth eyebrows rose, leaving little white crinkles cutting into his tanned skin.

"I'll let you make that decision." That should be enough to stop him from taking that job.

Now, time for one more argument. "You want your future charity, the equestrian camp for foster kids, to receive more donations, don't you? I can create a great website for you. Plus, I have excellent marketing skills." She reached into her pocket and placed her business card in front of him. "Check out my references if you don't believe me."

He palmed the card and studied it.

Was that respect or interest in his eyes? Hopefully, both.

Then he grimaced. "Okay, I see what I'd be getting. But I'm rough around the edges. I'm not easy to be around. I'm not marriage material. Don't you remember how my marriage ended, and in that case, I…"

He didn't finish the sentence. He'd loved her sister with a passion. He didn't love Heather. She needed a distraction. She poured more coffee.

"You're pouring past the rim."

"Oh. Oops." She swabbed the liquid with a dishrag, and a nervous giggle escaped.

"Huh. When you smile, you're actually…"

Her head jerked up as his voice trailed off again. Actually…? "What?"

"Never mind. What happens if I don't accept your offer?"

"I might… disappear." She was bluffing, but he didn't need to know it. "No freshly cooked food, groceries waiting in the fridge… Um, do you remember what happened when I took a vacation?"

He tapped the card against the table until the rhythm grew annoying. "Landon ran off three babysitters. He'd acted out so much, the only daycare facility in town refused to accept him. We lived on takeout from the restaurant. Hmm… I imagine you'd want separate bedrooms."

Was he considering it?

She inhaled and forgot to exhale.

Wait a moment.

Waaaaait a moment.

Bedrooms?

Heat sizzled through her again. "Of course. I'd rather sleep on the roof than in the same room with you. Or in another part of town. Or in the barn. Or—"

"Saying you want a separate bedroom would be enough. There are plenty of spare rooms in this house." He waved off the rest of her sentence before she could say she'd rather move to Alaska than sleep in the bedroom with him.

"Right." She picked up the skillet again. She needed to start that breakfast.

Then an idea occurred to her. Maybe to know how great—or at least tolerable—life with her would be he needed to know how bad life *without her* could be. "By the way, I'm taking a few days off. I have a project I need to complete as soon as possible."

Which was true. Besides, tomorrow was Saturday, Kade's day off, so she didn't feel too guilty.

His eyes widened.

Then he nodded. "Sure. But shouldn't a proposal involve a ring?" Teasing sparkles danced in his eyes.

Great.

He was having fun at her expense.

"Um, yeah." She rolled her eyes. That would be a normal proposal, and hers was anything but.

She searched around with her gaze and reached for the tie closing off the cellophane on the bread loaf. She handed it to Kade. "Here. Sorry I couldn't come up with anything better right now."

As his fingers touched hers when he accepted the "ring," her heart fluttered. Keeping her feelings in check around him would be difficult, but for Landon, she had to try.

He laughed. "Okay, I'll *think* about your proposal. Talk it over with my son. Let's see if he thinks life with you could be fun."

With her tummy knotting up, she wanted to take her words back, say she'd never meant them. Landon's laughter, followed by Dara's cheerful bark in the living room stopped her. She might not trust men any longer, but she still got attached easily.

"Of course, ask him." She turned on the skillet, waited for it to warm, and placed bacon on it.

Then she broke eggs into another skillet, going for a simpler breakfast because Kade needed to leave for work soon. He was on his phone now, answering a call from the ranch and probably forgetting her and her proposal.

The mouthwatering scents spread in the air, and her thoughts drifted.

Once upon a time, while her sister had dreamed of fame and riches together with her mother—her sister's beauty their ticket out of poverty—little Heather had been left alone and forgotten. Nobody had pinned any expectations on the chunky girl with plain looks. She'd had two simple dreams then.

One—to become valued, appreciated, and needed. She'd achieved that with her computer skills. Virtually all the businesses in town called her when their computers froze up, and she'd landed some important clients with her web designing and software development in different parts of the United States.

The second dream had been more difficult. She'd wanted a husband, a child, a house so friendly it felt like it greeted you with a hug, and, at one point, four dogs—based on her large size, Dara could qualify. Heather had wanted a loving family where a mother would care about her child and a father wouldn't have to work long hours, something so different from her own. She'd never want Landon to go through what she'd gone through.

So, despite a stab of guilt, she didn't take her words back.

Surely, Kade would come back with a no the day after tomorrow, but at least she'd tried.

As she piled up his plate with food, she knew she wouldn't be able to swallow a bite.

Their married life might turn out fun or a disaster, but she'd better not tell him that.

The next day, Kade rolled down his truck's window to breathe fresh air from the vast and beautiful rolling hills of the Show Me State. He'd traveled to many places before he'd realized that this place was in his blood, the part of him that he could never let go.

Who'd think that he'd love being a rancher, cowboy, and business owner so much? Definitely not him. Gratitude warmed his chest as he gave thanks that the Lord had guided him back to Mending Hearts and Cowboy Crossing.

He pressed on the gas, eager to get home to his son from the city where he'd gone for tractor parts.

His son had a playdate with his five-year-old cousin at his oldest brother's place. Kade had used the free time to work on a few documents and help feed the horses. At least that gave him the chance to stop by his favorite, a bay Thoroughbred named Spirit. Now, his chore was a drive into town for some tractor parts.

Amazing how often things broke on a ranch. Car and tractor repairs were among many skills he'd picked up through the years, but he couldn't do much without the right parts.

Even as he drove, he received several calls on his hands-free phone from the ranch. After resolving those issues, he told the guys he was taking the afternoon off. His son deserved his undivided attention.

He slowed around the curve and chuckled.

What a ridiculous proposal from his sister-in-law!

The only reason he'd agreed to think about it was to spare Heather's feelings. Though she didn't seem to like him much, she was good for his son, and that mattered a lot to him. Besides, it took guts to ask him to marry her.

She did have a nice smile when she'd allowed herself to laugh. Something surprising and warm unraveled inside him.

Unlike his ex, who'd taken great efforts to stand out and had spent hours putting on makeup and selecting her outfit—he'd learned that her "I'll be ready in five minutes" needed to be multiplied by thirty-six—Heather had seemed to do everything to blend into the background. She'd even seemed to choose T-shirts that matched his walls. She'd always worn thick awkward glasses, oversized T-shirts, and baggy jeans as if she'd tried to hide behind a curtain, and her gaze signified the door between them was closed.

He knew better than to knock on the locked door and had left it alone. But she was different with his son, and the boy had taken a shining to her since day one.

Landon…

His stiff shoulders loosening, Kade called his brother on the hands-free, letting Mac know he'd be in town soon. And he talked to Landon, who'd become the meaning of his life.

After hanging up, he smiled, the tender feeling lingering while he braked and stopped at the four-way stop.

As he moved forward at the green light, a noise from the right made him jerk his head in that direction. An eighteen-wheeler was moving toward him at high speed, appearing oblivious to the red light.

What in the world?

His blood turning cold, he glanced back, relieved that there was no car behind him, then slammed in reverse.

But the eighteen-wheeler was approaching fast.

Too fast.

And it didn't look like it was going to stop.

Ice filled his veins.

Lord, please help me. What's going to happen to my son if I die?

CHAPTER TWO

AT NOON, Kade still trembled inside. That near-collision was a close call. Thankfully, he'd managed to reverse in time, or that eighteen-wheeler running the red light would have steamrollered him.

He drew a deep breath as cold sweat slicked on his forehead. He was home now. He was with his precious boy. He was fine.

But what would happen to Landon if…

No, he shouldn't think like that.

He bounced his child, threw him in the air—carefully!—caught him, but while it usually elicited a delighted squeal, the usual trick didn't help.

The boy had messed with his breakfast instead of eating, and now sulked, refusing to do any of his regular activities. Dara, as if sensing the change of mood, huddled under the bed—not an easy feat for a dog her size—and stayed there.

Kade cringed. "What's wrong, kid? Why are you acting like this?"

Maybe his son just missed Heather. Strangely enough, even Kade felt some void after having her as a permanent fixture in his life.

Well, he also had a void for a different reason.

Taking care of the ranch, driving to the city and back, and studying Heather's website from the business card had made him skip two meals. Her work was so impressive he'd lost himself exploring websites she'd created. And when he'd called her references, everybody gushed about her work.

Huh.

Okay, he started seeing her in a new light.

A little.

"Let's go play with building blocks, okay?" He placed his son on the plush carpet and handed him a blue building block. Blue blocks were his son's favorites. The same bright color as Heather's eyes…

Where did that thought come from?

Landon studied the block, then threw it at him. "I don't wanna!"

"Someone is getting cranky." Kade held in a groan. "And by that, I mean myself. How does your auntie H make taking care of you look so easy?"

He'd done it without her help in California while his ex had been busy going to auditions, though it had been difficult. Today just wasn't his day.

His brother told him the boy refused any kind of breakfast or mid-morning snack he'd been offered, which meant Landon would be even crankier and hungrier by lunchtime. The lunch Heather had made for him last night and left in the fridge. Kinda thoughtful of her.

Huh.

Why hadn't he noticed such important details before?

He turned on his son's favorite cartoons and lifted him onto the sofa, placing the large toy dog near him. "I'll be right back. I need to check on the laundry."

The boy pouted. "Why don't you wanna marry Auntie H?

Then she could be here with me forever and ever. She's nice. And she makes the best pancakes ever!"

How could he explain that those weren't good enough qualifications for marriage?

Though his stomach did perk up at the mention of her pancakes. Mmm. Especially with raspberries and maple syrup.

No distraction!

"It's complicated, buddy." He tousled his son's hair.

His son looked at him and sighed.

"Aren't we happy, just the two of us?" He touched the tip of his son's nose, doing his best to sound cheerful.

His son sighed again. "Yeah, but all the kids have a mommy. I want one, too."

His chest constricted. He'd done the best he could, but it wasn't enough. "Not all kids. Your cousin doesn't."

Maybe this wasn't fair, especially considering that five-year-old had run off any potential mommies after babysitting her for a day. Most of the time it hadn't taken a day.

"She doesn't have anyone like Auntie H. Auntie H would be a good mommy. What if she marries someone else and has to be some other kid's mommy instead?" His little fingers fisted, and his lower lip stuck out.

He ruffled his son's hair and infused his voice with confidence he didn't feel. "She'll return tomorrow. You'll see."

Wouldn't she?

"I'll be back soon, bud." Kade straightened out.

Dara seemed to decide it was safe to venture out and joined the boy on the couch. His face still sad, Landon wrapped his arms around the big dog's neck. It tugged at Kade beyond measure.

After rushing to the laundry machine, Kade opened it and palmed his face. The groan he'd been holding back whooshed through his fingers.

Just great.

How could he remember minute details about the ranches, like the name of each Thoroughbred, or when to cut hay again, but not remember to check his pockets? Two pens managed to paint most of his white T-shirts and Landon's little white socks.

Could've been worse. He could've washed his phone.

And at least he separated whites from colors, right?

He'd been through much worse things in life than having to buy new T-shirts, though some of the ones he'd ruined were his favorites. He knew how to do laundry, did it all the time, but today he'd been so preoccupied with Landon and the near accident, and the ranch calls that still wouldn't stop coming, despite it being his day off.

He took a deep breath and stilled.

Something was wrong.

Dara ran to him, barking. Wait a moment—that wasn't a cheerful bark. This was a warning bark.

Oh no.

He sniffed the air. "Where's that smell coming from?"

Dara whined a little as if to trying to say it wasn't her fault.

"No, I don't mean you." Something was burning. This couldn't be happening. "I forgot that I put lunch in the oven!"

He did set the timer, didn't he?

Or had he forgotten?

The shrieking fire alarm gave him an unwelcome reply.

He raced to the kitchen, accompanied by Landon's screams and Dara's barks. Once there, he switched off the oven, then opened the windows and turned on the air conditioner. The alarm's shrill continued to flood the room. By the time he managed to reset it, the fire-truck siren sounded in the distance, most likely called by one of his caring neighbors.

Half an hour and an embarrassing explanation to the fire brigade later, plus about thirty calls from concerned Cowboy Crossing citizens, he played Frisbee on the lawn while the house aired out.

This was an accident.

It was okay.

Like he'd repeated many times to many people today, he hadn't burned the house down. One would think he'd had a near-death experience the amount of concern they'd poured out on him.

Near-death experience?

For the second time in one day?

He missed the catch while his gut tightened, and the Frisbee landed on the grass.

Was God telling him something?

If I die, what is going to happen to my son?

Kade had never thought about it before, really. And he knew the family would step in. But so would his ex. Not because she'd want to take care of the boy. But because she'd use him as a bargaining tool to get whatever she'd wanted from his family. And she'd want a lot.

Then there was the matter of Kade's con artist birth father…

"Daddy, send it back!" his darling boy yelled.

Kade obeyed, his mind whirling as fast as the Frisbee. If the boy had a mother who adopted him, his ex or the child's grandfather wouldn't have any ground. And it would be easier for Landon to survive the grief.

Now, what woman loved Landon as much as a mother should? What woman did Landon love equally?

The answer was simple.

Kade shook his head to his strange thoughts and looked around at the place that had always soothed his rough edges and kept him anchored.

The scent of grass filled the air, and as he breathed it in, hope expanded in his chest. He'd never get tired of his son's laughter.

Or of the view of the hunter-green rolling hills specked by emerald-hued trees, divided by white fencing, and accentuated by the tall red barn and grazing cows. From his house on the hill, he could even see the mirror-smooth surface of the spring-fed pond where his son loved to fish.

Nostalgia stirred inside Kade. He'd never expected to fall in love with this land. He'd stayed for Landon, to give him stability and a chance to be close to his grandmother, doting uncle and aunts, and an adorable cousin—and, yes, even his ex's father.

Kade had resented staying in one place then, balked over being tied down, and craved freedom. It had seemed as impossible as tying down the wind.

In the beginning, he'd felt like a fraud among this small town's hardworking people and his responsible family members. With biological parents like his, it was no surprise.

Though the Clark family had adopted him as a teen, he didn't feel any right to their wealth. So he'd started as a ranch hand, despite their protests, and worked his way up. He'd taken college courses and, later, studied agriculture online. Even with a small son, one could accomplish so much with determination and zero social life.

These days, he could ride along green fields feeling the wind on his skin, stare at the blue sky with cotton-like clouds, and wonder at just how blessed he was. He'd found unexpected freedom in the openness of these rolling hills, in the wind that hugged him like a friend, and in the promise for tomorrow that smelled like freshly cut grass.

Sometimes, though, part of him felt like this wasn't his identity, like he was destined for something else in a different place. Usually, it had happened after his biological father's texts, like today.

Kade's gut twisted. Maybe he shouldn't have agreed to let his father back into his life. Maybe it was a huge mistake.

Kade repeated something he'd told himself almost enough times to believe.

It wasn't just about forgiveness or about a midlife crisis like his older—and wiser—brother had hinted. It was about finding himself, even if at thirty-eight.

Or, like his sister Liberty beautifully put it, about being a total moron who didn't know what was good for him.

The leopard doesn't change his spots. You're more like me than you realize. People like us can't be tied down to one place, one person. You'll see.

His biological father's words rang in Kade's ears, making his stomach clench.

Was it about finding himself or being afraid of what he'd find? Genetics mattered, and he knew it well. He wouldn't expect an Appaloosa to turn into a Thoroughbred, would he?

"Daddy, I'm hungry." Landon's lower lip stuck out.

"Sorry, buddy." Oops, he shouldn't have let his thoughts venture away. "Let's go back." It should be all aired out by now. "What would you like for lunch?"

"Scrambled eggs with ham, onions, and peppers. The way Auntie H makes." The kid brightened as he rushed inside the house.

"I made you scrambled eggs for breakfast before taking you to your uncle's place. You didn't eat them." Kade followed his son, lifted Dara, and washed her paws in the bathroom.

"You didn't make them with enough peppers like she does." Landon held out Dara's towel.

Kade swallowed the comment that some hungry kids would be grateful for scrambled eggs without any peppers.

Ask him how he knew.

He and Landon marched to the kitchen, and as the kid climbed onto a chair, Kade gave him a large sheet of paper and crayons to pass the time while he cooked, as well as a few orange slices in a bowl to stave off the boy's hunger till lunch was ready.

Then Kade cut peppers on the counter, their fresh scent

invigorating the air and mingling with the citrusy one.

No, he'd never tell his son about the things he'd experienced as a kid. His son anchored him to this place, to this land, to something good and solid inside himself, and to his adoptive family that—shockingly!—loved him.

A warm feeling spread in his chest as he cut onions *fast*—no need for a grown man to cry—their pungent scent adding to the peppery aroma, then placed ham on the counter.

But an unease tightened his gut again, and he couldn't pinpoint why.

Oh, Heather's proposal.

He'd had women chasing after him before, but to propose? He chuckled. As ridiculous as it was, it gave him a pleasant feeling.

"Auntie H ain't gonna leave us, Daddy?" Worrisome notes in his son's voice put him on guard.

"Of course not." He infused his words with confidence. She might if he didn't accept her silly offer. "Today is her day off."

"I miss her." His son pouted again.

"It's only a few hours." Kade took an egg to break it, but somehow it slipped from his hands and ended up on the floor.

"Oh, I'll help." Landon jumped from his chair.

"No, please don't."

But his son already scooped up the eggy goop and eggshell from the floor and held his hands so close to his T-shirt that the mess ended up on it instead. Well, not all the mess.

The rest slid to his socks and sneakers.

"Oops, Daddy."

Sure enough, Dara decided to join in the fun, rushing into the kitchen.

"Dara, stop!" Kade lifted his hand in the universal stop sign.

Too late.

The dog slipped on the tile, slid forward, hit a table leg, and ended up wearing the bowl with oranges.

Crouching low on her belly, she whined apologetically.

Kade cringed at the mess and the two baths now necessary, one for the kid and one for the pet. But he smiled and reassured, for his son's and his dog's sakes. As a rescue, poor Dara had been sensitive, as if afraid they might return her to the animal shelter if she did something wrong.

"It's okay. I'll clean it up." He watered a paper towel, then leaned to the tiled floor and started cleaning. "And yeah, I miss her, too." The latter words he said quietly, almost unable to believe himself.

Apparently, Landon also anchored him to Heather, whether he wanted it or not. Kade frowned as he removed the bowl from the dog's head and told her to stay.

Maybe, just maybe, he needed Heather to stay, too. She made their lives better—and so much easier.

He received the proof of it when he tried to bathe the dog. Usually, she'd helped him with that, and Dara had obediently followed her to the bathroom.

Not today.

Dara dug in with all fours and whined.

He swallowed. "Well, then I'll have to carry you."

He lifted the dog who turned out even heavier than he'd guessed. The pet wiggled and whined until he put her down.

"She doesn't wanna a bath." Landon giggled.

"No kidding." Maybe showering her with a garden hose would work better? Kade could towel her dry before letting her back into the house.

He opened the door to the patio, and Dara squealed in delight and shot outside.

Great.

He snatched a few towels, and then his son followed.

"Landon, please stay out of the way." Kade placed the towels on the bench.

That did not work well. First, the boy chased the dog, then the dog chased the boy, and after a while, Kade couldn't say who was chasing whom.

"Stay! Both of you." He used the sternest voice he could find.

The boy and the dog froze as if a movie was put on pause. But sure enough, when he turned on the water and tried to water the dog down, apparently, he pressed the play button.

Kade groaned. His groan became louder when the dog ran to the sandbox where Landon used to play.

"Noooo!"

The dog didn't listen, and neither did his son. How come he could manage a ranch and many employees, but not his own pet or his son?

The wet dog rolled in the sand, obviously delighted.

"Daddy, look at me!" Landon did the same.

As Kade stared at the mud-covered dog and nearly mud-covered kid, he missed Heather with a passion. One would think she was a dog whisperer with the easy way Dara obeyed her.

Still, his disastrous first marriage had made him commitment-shy. And didn't Heather deserve a husband who loved her? He'd planned to pretend he thought about it, just long enough not to hurt her feelings with outright refusal, and then tell her no tomorrow.

After giving two baths—he'd never realized how long the way could be from the patio to the bathroom when one carried a large, wriggling dog—washing the floor, and getting his son into clean clothes, Kade scrambled eggs with peppers, ham, and onions in the kitchen.

The yummy scents spread through the room, but this time there was not enough ham, according to his son, while Auntie H always made it just right.

After lunch, he changed Landon's T-shirt again, as the kid was wearing a lot of peppers and onions by now, and kissed his hair. "What would you like to do now?"

The boy lifted his eyes to the ceiling. "I wanna play in the treehouse."

"Sure, buddy. Want me to take a book to read to you?"

"Yes. My favorite."

Kade waited, but his son didn't continue. "Um, which one is your favorite?"

The boy sighed, which clearly stated Auntie H would know. "About a puppy."

They climbed onto the large oak in the yard and inside the treehouse Kade had built, and he breathed in the scent of fresh air and leaves. The oak was one of many other things that had signified a legacy that would stay here long after him, a legacy to pass to his son. Birds chirruped in the branches, and the sun gently caressed foliage with its rays.

What would have happened to Kade if he'd never shown up at this ranch? Most likely, he'd be dead or in prison. Landon would never have existed.

He winced, then thanked God for bringing him here as he started reading to his son.

After Kade said "The End," and closed the book, peace and calmness entered him.

He was a good parent.

He could do this.

"I wanna go back. Getting too hot in here." Landon climbed outside first.

For a second, worry tightened Kade's heart, but his son had climbed trees and ladders since he'd been very little.

Kade, on the other hand, didn't have that much experience. His foot slipped from the ladder step, and he gasped.

"Daddy!" His son's frightened scream reached his ears.

He was going to fall!

CHAPTER THREE

TODAY WAS NOT HIS DAY.

"I'm okay, buddy. I'm okay." Kade got up from the grass and hugged his son, whose lower lip was trembling.

His adoptive father had taught him how to fall while riding a horse, and that was a useful skill. Something he needed to pass to his son, too.

Kade assessed himself for injuries. But apart from a few bruises, nothing seemed dislocated or broken, and he sent up a prayer of gratitude. While his relationship with God was complicated, he'd tried to be a good Christian, partly because it was a legacy, too, to pass to his boy.

Kade's phone rang when they'd come back inside, while he was helping his son construct something between a multiple-car garage or a castle from building blocks.

He suppressed a groan. He loved his job, he really did now, but not another call from the ranch!

As he fished his phone out of his back pocket and glanced at the screen, the name evoked mixed feelings. On one hand, joy over talking to his adoptive mother, but on the other hand, irritation over the likely reason for her call. Had she already heard about his mishap with the fire alarm while in a different state?

Actually, her timing wasn't bad, considering how much he needed advice from the person he trusted the most. The person who'd been the matriarch of the family business after becoming a widow too young and had helped her sons and daughter make a barely surviving ranch a profitable one, then added more ranches, more buildings, more cattle. Someone wise and patient was what he needed right now.

Especially considering this concerned her future daughter-in-law. He hadn't asked for her advice for his first marriage, and sometimes he'd been afraid she and the previous daughter-in-law he'd given her would do bodily harm to each other if he didn't referee.

Exhaling, he swiped the screen to answer, then added another cube to Landon's construction. "I'm glad you called. I, um, have a situation here."

His stomach tightened. At first, he'd been rebellious when adopted, but once he'd realized his mother wasn't going to leave him like his birth parents had, he'd grown to love her more than he'd wanted to admit and to seek her approval.

She'd never shown him, but he'd undoubtedly disappointed her many times, including when he'd married Josephine and when he'd divorced.

Little wonder something roiled in the pit of his stomach.

"Are you okay? Is Landon okay?"

A sting jabbed him over her alarm. "We're okay. Sorry, didn't mean to worry you. I, um, there was a marriage proposal, and..."

She groaned. "You're getting married again?"

He could read her thoughts. *Didn't you learn anything the first time around?*

This wasn't going well.

At all.

"Think how it's going to affect Landon." She adored the boy

as if Landon had been her biological grandson, that much Kade knew.

He could imagine her in his mind's eye, concern in those blue eyes that never became faded, a bob of gray hair feathering around her kind face. She'd always worn the pearl earrings her husband had given for their tenth anniversary. When she'd lost one earring days after his death, she'd continued to wear the other.

Kade had wanted to buy her a new set until he'd realized, probably like everyone else in the family, that some things couldn't be replaced.

"My son is why I might consider getting married again." He resisted the urge to grind his teeth, then snatched a plush dog toy and handed it to the boy.

Landon jumped. "Daddy, you're gonna get married to Auntie H then! Thank you! Thank you! Thank you!" He threw his little hands around Kade's neck, then snatched the large toy dog from the sofa and started dancing with it. "Hurrah! Hurrah! Hurrah!"

Kade's heart dropped into the plush carpet. He should've had this conversation in private. He was getting too distracted today and not thinking things through.

"I said, I *might* consider it. Might. Consider," he said softly to his boy.

"Oh." His son plunked on the carpet, grimacing.

"Are you there? What happened?" The voice on the phone made him return to the conversation.

"Yes, I'm here."

"I'm just concerned about you. Your first marriage put you through the wringer."

Well, this was his answer. Bad enough he'd upset her when he'd married Josephine. He wasn't going to do it again. He'd say no to Heather tomorrow and get this over with.

Disappointment surprised him.

It was what he wanted, wasn't it?

"Okay, okay. I'm not going to interfere with your life." Her voice softened. "I imagine you love this girl very much. Who is she?"

"Heather Johnson. And I don't love her. I mean, she's a good person, and I respect her and trust her, and… Well, she proposed. I don't know why or how this crazy idea came to her mind, but—"

"Wait. What? Heather?" Her screech rattled the speaker. "Praise God! Quick, marry that girl before she comes to her senses and changes her mind."

Seriously?

His jaw slackened. "Excuse me?"

If he hadn't been so confident, that would hurt his ego. As Landon got bored with the plush toy, instead the kid's numerous cars came into play, as he drove them around and then into the block tower.

Kade cleared his throat. "Huh. Well… I guess that means you're giving me your blessing."

"I'm giving you a thousand blessings. A million blessings! It's okay that you don't love her yet. You will once you get to know her. My marriage to your father was arranged, but I couldn't wish for a better man and loved him with all my heart. I–I always will."

"I know. I love and miss him, too." His adoptive father passed away years ago and had been present in Kade's life for only three years. But still, surprisingly intense pain tightened his stomach. Maybe more for the hurt his death had caused the family he'd grown to love than for his own hurt, especially for his mother. He'd never seen two people love each other more than his adoptive parents. "The thing is…I don't need to get to know her. I've known her for years."

First, because she was best friends with his sister. Then, because he'd married Heather's sister. And now, because she'd helped with Landon.

Granted, she had kindness in her blue eyes, but those eyes

29

were usually hidden behind thick glasses. Otherwise, there was nothing spectacular about her. She always wore baggy dull clothes, pinned her braid at the nape of her neck, and looked down when she'd talked to him as if he either made her uncomfortable or she'd never tolerate his company if it wasn't for her nephew.

"Yes, you've seen her taking care of Landon, but do you really know her? You might not realize what a treasure you have in front of your eyes." Each sentence came out stronger. "Okay, I need to start a prayer chain. Hold on. My sister's entered the room. I gotta share this with her, okay?"

"Okay." His aunt wasn't a gossiping kind and had a good head on her shoulders. Plus, after visiting Cowboy Crossing often, she'd met Heather. Most likely, his aunt would say this was a crazy idea, and that would be it.

He occupied himself creating another cube construction with Landon, a bridge under which the toy cars could run. Tenderness expanded his chest as he ruffled his son's soft hair.

As the boy scowled, swatted at his hair on his forehead, and scooted out of reach—his sulky mood apparently returned—Kade's mother came back on the line. "Well, my sister said I was wrong."

Just like he'd expected. Then why did his stomach tighten again? He didn't want this ridiculous marriage.

Or did a small—very, very, very small—part of him want it?

"Yes," she continued. "I was wrong. She said, in this case, starting one prayer chain isn't enough. She's going to call everyone she knows and ask them to pray for an improbable cause."

He groaned, and yet... that tiny part of him perked up. "You can't be serious."

"I'm serious. Oh, and I'm returning to Cowboy Crossing tomorrow. Somebody needs to prepare this wedding and make sure the girl doesn't escape." No point arguing when she used her do-your-homework-now voice. "I know why you're so reluctant to give this a chance. You're afraid this marriage will end like your first one. But Heather is different from her sister. She's not going to walk away."

"I'm afraid *I* will!" The words exploded from him. Then he hushed his tone as he glanced at his son. He really should've had this conversation in private. He was making bad decisions today. "Like you said, Heather is a good person. I don't want to hurt her."

A tug pulled at his heart, so it wasn't because he didn't want to lose a great babysitter and cook. "You know the way I am. I... don't stick around. I... was made that way, I guess."

"Give yourself more credit, Horse Whisperer. And give this marriage a chance."

She hadn't called him that since he was a teen. Feeling as if she'd just covered him with a warm blanket like she'd done so many times in his troubled teens, he talked to her some more, then hung up.

Several hours later, he persuaded himself this would never work. As his son watched cartoons and Kade tried to salvage what he could from the laundry, another incoming call made him wince.

He pulled out the phone from his jeans pocket and smiled. His rough-around-the-edges sister would surely side with him. Liberty knew he wasn't made for marriage. Besides, she wouldn't wish her best friend a spouse who wasn't keen on commitment.

"Hello, sis." Her image, complete with her emerald-green short-cut hair, almost always covered by a Stetson, flashed in his mind.

"Okay, the family just voted." How like her not to waste time on pleasantries.

"Voted on what?" He wrinkled his forehead. Had he somehow missed some new acquisition vote?

"On whether you should marry Heather. We've got ten votes, all for it."

Despite the ridiculousness, he chuckled. "That's impossible. There are four adult people in the family besides me."

Well, there were two more, but they hadn't chosen to live on the ranch. His older sister had traveled as far as Europe and never looked back. And his other brother Maverick preferred the career of a car racer to the one of a rancher.

"Everybody voted with both hands. Well, everybody besides me."

While he should be offended that his adoptive family tried to decide his life, at least he knew he had Liberty's support. "So you voted against it, right? Wait. The numbers still don't add up. There should be six votes for it and one against it."

"It's ten for it because I took off my boots and voted with my hands *and* my feet."

A cross between a laugh and an angry snort burst from his mouth. "You're kidding me."

"I would never kid with the happiness of my brother and my best friend." She paused. "Wait a moment. I'm sure I'm going to be a maid of honor—do all maids of honor have to wear a dress?"

This might be his chance. "If we don't marry, you won't have to wear a dress."

"For Heather, I'll wear a dress."

This was big.

What a difference from his first marriage when Liberty had the escape car ready and did her best to talk him into canceling the ceremony until the last possible minute.

He talked about the ranch matters with her, then hung up and walked to the living room. Laundry would wait.

Lord, I want what's best for my son. Please guide me. I want to make sure he has a good future, even if I'm not here to take care of him. All that is happening today, barely avoiding being hit by an eighteen-wheeler, nearly burning the kitchen, and falling from a tree... Is this a sign I should consider Heather's proposal? Is this

Your guidance?

Kade sat on the sofa and leaned to his son. "Buddy, so do you want Aunt H to come to live here for some time?"

"Yay, Daddy!" His son brightened and clapped, then went in for a hug. "We're gonna be a family! Yay! Hurrah! Yay! Hurrah!"

His heart shifted as he hugged the boy. This was making Landon happy.

But the marriage still didn't make sense.

His phone rang again, and something warmed inside him when he saw Heather's name on the screen. He swiped it to answer with an eagerness he didn't expect. "Hello, Heather."

"Are you okay? Is Landon okay?"

"I guess you heard about the fire alarm. We're fine." He wanted to tell her to come back today, but it wouldn't be fair. She more than deserved time off.

A sigh of relief traveled down the line. "Oh great. Did you like the lunch I left you?"

"Um, that was what caused that fire alarm in the first place." His fingers tightened around the phone as if it were her hand.

Wait a moment.

Did he want to hold her hand?

"Oh. Oooooh. Well, do you need me to come over and cook something for you?"

His impatience to say yes surprised him. "No, you deserve to rest. Landon misses you, though."

He missed her, too, for the first time. But he couldn't even comprehend that fact, much less share it.

"I miss him, too." Her voice softened, and he imagined her blue eyes softened behind those thick lenses, too.

Did she miss *him*? His pulse increased a little, another surprise at the jolt he had for the answer to be affirmative.

Would their marriage just be a business arrangement for her, or had she developed feelings for him while he wasn't looking?

Did he want her to?

His pulse increased even more. This was all so confusing.

Probably the pause stretched because she drew a shaky breath and said, "I'll see you both tomorrow. Just wanted to make sure you are fine."

"Thanks." He stared at the screen for some time after she disconnected.

Was he fine, though? A myriad of thoughts rushed through his head, and different feelings assailed him.

Late in the evening, he tucked his son in bed and read him a story.

"I'm gonna sleep. Then I wake up, and Auntie H will already be here." The boy grinned.

"Yes, she will be." He read a part of another story and watched his boy's eyelids close.

Would she leave if he didn't accept her ultimatum?

Kade paced the living room for an hour or so. Then he walked into Landon's room to check on him and smiled as his son snuggled in his bed, hugging his favorite plush puppy in his sleep.

A toy Heather had given him.

Landon was wearing his *bestest* pajamas with a puppy pattern, and a peaceful smile curved his adorable face. Kade grinned, remembering how Heather had bought a matching set of PJs so they could pretend she was a mamma dog and Landon was her, well, puppy. She'd even barked, and Landon had imitated her in a fun sound.

Landon would be happy with her.

That was plain and simple.

Tenderness, love, and worry squeezed Kade's heart as he watched his treasure. His birth parents had abandoned him, and after he'd tracked down his history, he'd realized it had been for the best.

He shuddered at the memory of the things that had happened

to him when he'd been a child.

If something happened to him, orphaning his son... Kade closed his eyes and opened them.

Of course, Mom or Liberty would take Landon in a heartbeat, but what if Josephine decided to claim the child out of spite or to see how much she could get from his family?

It wasn't just about his ex trying to blackmail his family with the boy. His birth father would use the opportunity when he saw it. He wasn't a great con artist for nothing.

Bottom line—Kade wanted his son to have a mother. A loving mother who'd adore him. This marriage would also make Mom and Liberty happy.

If he said yes, he'd make three people he loved with his whole heart happy. He covered his son with a cuddly blanket and kissed the soft hair on the top of the boy's head, his chest expanding.

As he tiptoed out of his son's room, his mind whirled.

For a man like him, who had abandonment and commitment issues, marriage would be a tall order. If he couldn't make it work with the woman he'd once loved, how could he make it work with a woman he didn't love at all?

Lord, what should I do?

His faith was fragile at best, but his adoptive family had taught him to pray, had taught him to believe. He hadn't been a great Christian, had made his fair share of mistakes, but he'd been trying so hard to do better since his son was born.

For the rest of the night, Kade tossed and turned, only to succumb to nightmares of his broken childhood.

In the morning, he prayed again. He could hardly believe the answer that formed in his mind.

He swallowed as he picked up the phone and stared at the screen.

It was time.

"Good morning. I hope I didn't wake you." When she

answered, he spoke fast, afraid he'd change his mind. "I thought a lot about your proposal, and the answer is yes. I mean, for Landon, I'll give this a try."

Just great. He grimaced. Who gave marriage *a try*?

A loud thud juddered on the other end of the line.

Whoa. His rib cage constricted.

Had Heather dropped her phone, or had she fainted?

CHAPTER FOUR

FOUR DAYS LATER, Heather stared out the window at the green rolling hills beyond the pristine white limousine speeding her up to the house of her—gasp!—husband. The leather seats' scent mixed with his enticing cologne and made her head spin. Okay, so maybe her head had been spinning since he'd said yes to her proposal.

Had he lost his mind?

Had both of them lost their minds?

Her thoughts in turmoil, she rubbed her throbbing temples and didn't dare to look at Kade sitting beside her.

How did this happen?

Okay, she knew how this had happened. She'd been there when she'd proposed. But she was fulfilling a promise to her dad. She was sure Kade, one of the most eligible bachelors in Cowboy Crossing, would say no.

It wasn't that she'd grown up poor and he belonged to one of the most influential families in town, even if by adoption and not birth. He'd married her sister, after all, so he hadn't worried about social status.

But in the looks and outgoing personality department, on the scale from one to ten, he was a thousand, and she was... an optimistic three.

On a good day.

Her fingers twitched to pinch herself hard enough to make sure this wasn't a dream. She'd wanted a family since she'd been little.

Maybe she shouldn't have drunk that glass of champagne at the reception because it must be affecting her too much. She hadn't eaten the entire day, afraid her queasy stomach might let her down and return the food—probably somewhere on Kade's dashing tuxedo.

The last time she'd drunk... Well, she didn't remember the last time that had happened, so the champagne must've gotten to her.

Yes, that must be the reason.

When the limousine stopped and Kade opened the door for her, she stumbled out on unsteady feet. Still avoiding looking at him, she sized up the distance to the porch and up the stairs. *How* was she going to make it if she was staggering?

As she suppressed a groan, her shoulders drooped.

Kade scooped her up. "It's a tradition to carry the bride across the threshold of her new home."

Wide-eyed, she gawked at him.

The spinning didn't stop. If anything, it became stronger. She'd been wrong. She wasn't drunk on champagne.

She was drunk on Kade.

Her skin heated up, more from the warmth inside than the Missouri summer sunshine. When she looked in his dark eyes, breathed in his cologne, she wanted to forget this was only a business arrangement.

A contract, really, like the ones she did for her job.

He made a few steps forward, his muscles bulging.

Uh-oh.

Embarrassment added to the heat of excitement. While she

wasn't *hugely* overweight, she was on the plump side. Something about her constitution made her gain weight easily, and fine, she'd been a comfort eater, too.

It was so unfair. Her sister could inhale a cake and not gain an ounce. But if Heather as much as smelled a cake in a fifty-mile radius, it all went to her hips and waist.

So compared to her sister, she was more than plump. But then compared to her sister a stick would look like an elephant.

"Um, I might be a bit heavy," she whispered.

He staggered forward. "You're fine."

"Maybe that tradition worked for skinny brides like my sister. As for me, well, fat cells had an agreement to leave my sister's body and make a home on mine."

"You're funny." He chuckled as he made another step forward.

Oh boy.

"That's not a good idea," she told her husband—seriously, husband!—at the same time as she wound her arms around his neck.

Her heart was beating so fast it seemed it would break her rib cage.

"I've got you." His breath caressed her skin.

Well, she couldn't try to wiggle her way out of his arms, could she? Like Landon when someone he didn't like—like his biological mother—tried to hug him.

Uh-oh.

Her pulse increased if that was even possible. Her mother-in-law—wow!—had taken her grandson for a few days "to give the newlyweds some privacy." Heather was used to having the child as a buffer.

To be with Kade alone in the house—even if in different rooms—she couldn't grasp that.

That was, if they made it to that house. She wasn't easy to

carry. Good thing he'd worked out in the gym and his muscles were also chiseled by many hours of manual labor. Many other guys would've collapsed after the first step.

Correction.

Other guys wouldn't even try.

After three of his somewhat wobbly steps, she promised herself to give up French fries. After another three—pastries. When he stopped before the white porch—chocolate.

No, not chocolate.

Let's not get too crazy here.

"You should put me down," she said. "Really."

"I'm not going to drop you." Something changed in his voice. Was there surprise and tenderness, or was it her wishful thinking? "I'll never want to drop you."

Was it his way of saying "I'll stand by you?"

Yeah right.

Now *that* was wishful thinking! Everyone knew Kade was a player. Early or late, he'd get tired of her and leave.

She nearly snorted. He wasn't even attracted to her yet, so no worrying about him getting tired of her.

Her eyes widened at the garlands of white roses decorating the railings, their fragrance welcoming her, and large posters on the windows flinging out the word *Congratulations*. Bright balloons, tied to the posts of the wraparound porch, flapped in the air.

"You did all that?" she asked as he opened the door.

"My brother and sister helped, and so did my son." He grinned at her. "We wanted you to feel welcome."

That grin made her heart blossom like the flowers on the porch.

He'd made an effort when he didn't have to. And he'd insisted on paying for the reception at the best local restaurant, as well as the limousine, photographer, cake, live band, and many details she didn't even think of.

Maybe this was because of his family's status.

But she wanted to believe that in a small part it was because of her, too. She'd drawn the line at a honeymoon. Neither one of them wanted to leave Landon, and besides, what was the point when they'd be living in separate rooms?

One step.

A little rest.

Another one.

More rest.

Strain tightened his features.

She swallowed. The last thing she wanted was for his back to go out. Perfect start of married life. Not! "Um, you know, it's okay if you put me down."

"We're almost there."

As they entered the house, he didn't put her down with relief but stared into her eyes as if mesmerized.

Yeah right.

She tried for a light tone. "Well, this should count as a workout at the gym for a couple of days."

He chuckled, though his breathing was labored. "Yeah. I never noticed your sense of humor. Or how beautiful your eyes are. They are the color of the sky on a summer day. They are… luminous."

Her jaw dropped.

Nobody had ever told her that.

Okay, she needed to remind herself that giving compliments was part of his demeanor. She playfully swatted at his forearm. "Oh, stop it. I'm sure you told that to many girls."

"No. Only to you." His eyes grew serious.

No, no, no.

She could guard her heart when he didn't pay attention to her. But when he carried her in his arms, when he'd decorated the entrance with her favorite flowers, when he told her things like that and looked like he cared about her…

41

How was she supposed to guard her heart now?

"Put me down, please." She looked away.

This time he did as she'd asked.

She ran a hand along her simple white dress. "I need to change." She kept a few changes of clothes here in case she got dirty playing with Landon. "Then I can make you dinner."

"Thank you, but I'm not hungry. I ate plenty at the reception."

"Right." She shifted from one foot to the other.

Without cooking or taking care of Landon, what was she supposed to do? How to keep herself away from this man right in front of her who made her pulse skyrocket?

Oh yes!

She perked up. "I can start working on that website I promised you."

"Please. Not tonight. This is your wedding day." Surprise flared the edges of his eyes as if he couldn't believe he'd gotten married again.

"Right." Why'd she keep saying that? "Okay." Not much better, but it'd have to do.

She swallowed hard. Tonight was supposed to be their wedding night. Good thing they'd already agreed on separate rooms.

"Okay." Didn't she just say that, too? "I'll go change."

She'd said that, too.

She cringed. It was so much easier when there was none of this… awareness in the air. Why did she have to change that?

Thanks, Dad.

"Wait." He touched her hand, and something akin to an electric current—but a pleasant one—passed through her.

Then his eyes widened, and he moved his hand as if the touch affected him, too. "I mean, I know you're tired and want to rest, but… Would you like to do something?"

"Like what?" She should've thought about common interests

before that crazy proposal.

"Ride horses and watch the sunset?" His hip cocked out to the right, and his lips pinched together as he studied her.

To other people, that would sound romantic. But since a horse had bitten her... She shuddered.

Of course, he was a cowboy through and through, so what he'd suggested made sense to him. He loved horses. Everyone in town knew the equestrian ranch was his baby, and he'd probably sleep in the stables if not for his son.

"No thank you. How about watching a romantic comedy?" Oops, he liked action movies. "Oh, never mind."

"I can watch a romantic comedy." He snatched a remote control but didn't sound too enthusiastic.

"No, it's okay." Her heart sank.

His eyes lit up. "How about going for a jog? I know scenic trails in the park. We might even spot wildlife. Well, not today, but... someday."

Besides love for Landon, they had nothing in common. This marriage was doomed from the start.

She'd suffered temporary insanity when she'd suggested it.

Was she going to set the record for the shortest marriage in the county?

Now what?

CHAPTER FIVE

THIS WASN'T GOING WELL. Heather's first day being married, and she already thought how wrong they were for each other.

"Um, no thanks. I'm not into sports." Her heart sank even lower.

The only jogging she'd done was from Landon's room to the fridge for a snack and back. Amazing that, after a busy day on his feet and carrying her inside the house, he'd even consider jogging.

He looked at her, probably realizing he should've let her work on that website. "Well, you like marshmallows, right?"

She nodded. A cup of cocoa with marshmallows could be good at the computer. "I sure do. They are sweet and soft. Kind of like I am." She chuckled without mirth.

"Kind of like you are." From him, it sounded like a compliment. "How about roasting marshmallows over a fire? It's not cold outside."

Something warmed her as if she already sat near the fire. "That would be great."

Minutes later, after she'd changed into a light black sweater and gray pants and he'd changed into jeans and a T-shirt, they were sitting before the fire pit in his spacious backyard. Even here, garlands of white roses wove over the white picket fence where a long *Congratulations* sign stretched along the posts.

If she didn't know better, she could believe she'd just had a real wedding. Her heart squeezed as he built the fire. No point to wish for things that couldn't be.

He handed her a roasting stick, and she picked a marshmallow from the bag.

As she held it above the fire, tongues of flame licked the logs. "I want to thank you for what you've done. I know it wasn't easy."

"It was much easier than I thought it would be." He bobbed his marshmallow above the fire, too. "Besides, something tells me I got the better side of the deal. So no need to thank me." He tilted his head back. "When we were teens, Dad used to roast marshmallows over the fire with us. We'd take turns telling stories and jokes. And then he'd play the harmonica."

She could relate to loving a father beyond measure, and she was blessed to have hers still. "You must be missing him very much."

She wiggled her crispy marshmallow from its stick, blew on it to cool it down a bit, then munched on its gooey sweetness to chase away the bitterness in her mouth.

"I do." A faraway look glazed his eyes. "He taught me to play harmonica and gave me his. Not to either of his biological sons. But to me."

"You know he loved you as his own." She shifted closer. Her throat clogged up, but that must be from the smoke.

"I haven't been able to play it since his death." His voice dipped to barely a whisper.

She had to move closer still, wishing she could take his pain. "But you have it, just like you'll carry love for him forever."

"I do." He handed her his ready marshmallow, reached in his pocket, and pulled out a small harmonica. He looked at it for a long time, and she didn't say a word, was even afraid to breathe.

Then he brought it to his mouth and started to play.

She finished that melting marshmallow fast and placed the sticks aside to give her full attention to the tune. She wasn't a huge music fan—great, another thing they *didn't* have in common—but the depth of emotion in the tune tugged on her heart.

Beautiful and tender...so incredibly sad...

She wanted to cry and smile at the same time. Maybe smile through tears? It was the melody of someone who felt deeply and suffered greatly.

How could someone like Kade play like that?

Her image of him—an irresistible, easygoing player who'd never stayed long in one place or relationship, the image he'd presented to the world—morphed into the image she saw today, an image she couldn't make match up.

Granted, he'd turned out to be a responsible father when people least expected him to be and stayed in Cowboy Crossing after bringing Landon home from California. But what about that rumor he'd been looking for jobs in other places?

Then she stopped overanalyzing things, closed her eyes, and let the tune carry her away. To a faraway place where people truly loved each other, good people didn't finish last, and even she could be loved and treasured just the way she was.

Maybe that was her third, the most unattainable dream.

To be loved the way she was.

When the music stopped, she didn't want to open her eyes, didn't want to leave that magical land. A soft stroke over her fingers sent a pleasant wave spreading through her body, and she hung onto that feeling, even if only for moments.

As she opened her eyes, her mouth slackened. She had her head on his shoulder.

How... how did that happen?

And his hand covered hers.

Warmth spread through her, and she couldn't blame it on the

fire. Okay, maybe on the fire *inside* her and not in the fire pit. She slid away and removed her hand from his.

Did disappointment flash in his eyes?

Nah, she was seeing things.

She cleared her throat. "That was so… haunting. I didn't realize you had such talent. Who wrote it?"

"I did." His eyes became unreadable.

"Oh. For my sister, right?" Jealousy zapped her.

"No. I was just… remembering things."

"Remembering things?" She moved toward him as she breathed in the scent of smoke and burning wood, sensing pain and regret in his voice.

"I should've told you about all this before, well, before marriage. This town knows some of my history, but not all." He handed her the marshmallow bag.

She picked up the stick and skewered a marshmallow. "You don't have to tell me if you don't want to." Even as part of her held her breath, she pretended to focus on the bronzing gooey treat. "I mean, I know you were adopted if that's what you want to talk about."

Now his whole expression became hooded. "Do you know I have a juvenile record? That my birth parents were burglars? Well, my birth dad decided to become a con artist later on."

She gasped and dropped the marshmallow into the fire. It sizzled and smoked, tainting the air with something equal parts acrid and sweet. "I… didn't. But it wouldn't matter to me."

"It wouldn't?" Something inquisitive entered his gaze.

His eyes…

They drew her so much she was desperate to hug him, to kiss him, to prove with action her words.

Oh, to kiss him…

A delicious shiver ran through her, and it took all her willpower to stay away.

Taking another deep breath of smoke-scented air, she gathered her runaway thoughts. "What matters is who you are *now*. You're an awesome father. You're a great rancher. And look what an amazing job you did with the equestrian ranch in such a short time." She didn't add that this was the reason other ranch owners searched him out.

"Well, that's easy to do. I love Landon, and I love what I do. Plus, the family trusted me with the initial capital for my acquisitions."

"Considering your beginnings, it's even more impressive you managed to turn your life around. But if you want to tell me things... I am a good listener." Not being a talkative type herself helped in the latter. But in this case, she also wanted to know as much as possible about Kade.

She wanted to know *everything*.

Even if that would make it so much more difficult not to fall for him. She might be able to resist the easygoing player. She'd learned not to fall for the handsome shell.

But this...

She found his hand and laced her fingers through his to show her support.

"I was passed from one foster family to another. By fourteen, I knew very well that nobody wanted me. I wouldn't be adopted. The foster family where I landed made it clear they only had me for the income. I figured if they didn't need me, I didn't need them, either." His voice was void of emotion as if he were telling someone else's story.

"I'm so sorry," she whispered as her heart went out to him.

She nearly covered her mouth with her free hand. So much for being a good listener and not interrupting.

"I started doing chores for my neighbors. After a few months, I saved up, as I thought, enough. After my foster father yelled at me again, I ran away. Took their car, too. One of the older foster siblings had taught me to drive, and I turned out to be a natural. I followed the speed limit. Drove mostly at night while sleeping in the rest areas during the days. Bought food at gas stations. I ended up close to Cowboy Crossing because the car broke down nearby." He wrapped his fingers tighter around hers, and then he brought them to his lips.

As he kissed them one by one, she held her breath.

She couldn't take her hand away, not now, even if the tumultuous feelings scared her. And she wouldn't ask what happened next, no matter how much she wanted to know.

"I walked to the town since I was getting hungry. Then... then I saw this magnificent horse, a Thoroughbred stallion. I didn't know that horse belonged to one of the most influential families in town and wouldn't care if I did. I stole it. That was how I met my adoptive parents."

Her jaw slackened for the second time in the evening. "You stole their horse?"

"Yup. They found out where I was from and decided to return me to my foster family."

He paused.

"I was furious. I yelled things at them I never want to repeat or remember. When later they invited me to the ranch for the summer, I laughed so hard. But I figured, I had nothing to lose and might have a little revenge. It's nothing short of a miracle that, not only did they survive all my... antics but also they decided to adopt me."

"They saw the real you behind the hurting, acting-out boy," she didn't say it as a question but as a statement.

"I guess they did. The rest is history. And now you know."

She drew a deep breath of damp night air.

With the fire diminishing, the air felt colder, fresher.

Things made more sense now. He'd learned to be afraid of commitment, to avoid abandonment.

Maybe all his many relationships had ended fast because he needed to walk out on people before they walked out on him. Except for her sister, but look how that turned out. It confirmed his theory that he needed to leave before others left him.

Realizing it made her hurt more.

For him.

For herself.

For their doomed marriage.

"You were right." He studied her. "You're a great listener. You're easy to talk to. You're easy to be with. You're… incredible."

She blinked.

Then blinked again.

Another pleasant wave swept her up, and she hadn't even kissed him yet. During today's now-you-can-kiss-the-bride moment, she'd turned her cheek to him.

Okay, she needed to remind herself he was good at compliments. Excellent even. "Incredible? Please! I'm not like the other women you've dated."

"I'm thankful for that." He leaned toward her.

Despite their being out in the fresh air, breathing became difficult.

Think.

Think!

"I mean, I'm not your type. Those gorgeous blondes—" She didn't have a chance to add "with hourglass figures."

He interrupted her. "I love your hair." He plucked the pins and tiny flowers out of her bun and handed them to her.

Then he ran his fingers through her dark hair and breathed in deeply. "It's luscious and soft and smells of flowers with a hint of smoke flavor."

Okay. Wow.

What just happened?

He sniffed her hair.

Did he sniff her hair?

Okay. Wow.

She already thought that.

"It's my perfume. And well, smoke from the fire," she said when she finally found her tongue.

"Why do you always hide your eyes behind glasses?" He slid off her glasses.

Whaaat?

She blinked again. She seemed to be doing a lot of blinking lately. "Because I don't see well. Hello?"

Okay, maybe that wasn't too friendly, but she felt oddly vulnerable without her glasses.

He didn't point out she could've gotten contact lenses.

"I want to see your eyes better. And your skin… It's flawless." He ran his fingertips along her jaw, making her give out a tiny gasp.

Was he going to kiss her?

Her heartbeat went into overdrive, and another delicious shiver rushed through her.

"I'm sorry. You're cold, and I'm keeping you outside." He replaced her glasses and doused the fire. "Let's go back."

What?

How?

Why?

No!

She wasn't cold at all.

In fact, she needed a cold shower to calm her heartbeat and cool her heated skin. She glanced at the embers as she got up, and her rib cage constricted.

The evening was amazing, and she committed it to memory, as well as the feeling of his touch.

Her attraction to him was growing with every minute, but it

was no use. Even if she managed to create sparks inside him, they'd soon become what she saw in front of her.

Embers.

CHAPTER SIX

IN THE MORNING, Kade stared at Heather as she slept—not just because she'd mixed up the rooms yesterday and ended up in his bedroom instead of the guest room she'd chosen for herself. He'd spent the night on the living room couch because he didn't have the heart to wake her and point out her mistake.

No, the real reason was because there was something fascinating about watching people sleep. Maybe they were the most real in that moment.

Okay, those moments were, well, stolen. But then he'd been a thief once.

According to his biological father, Kade had been born a thief. Premonition squeezed his heart. He'd told the man he hadn't wanted him to visit this summer, but the guy hadn't cared. If the man showed up, how would he keep him away from his family?

Kade's curiosity about his heritage when he'd been twenty-five and finally agreed to see his biological father in between the guy's prison sentences had come with a high price tag.

He closed his eyes and opened them again. His father had met him in an upscale restaurant in St. Louis, and nothing had been as he'd expected.

Charismatic, cheerful, generous with tips and compliments to the waitress, he'd eaten his osso buco—Kade didn't even know then what that meant—with knowledge and appreciation, as well as crème brûlée, and ordered the glass of wine like a connoisseur.

The surreal experience somehow suited the restaurant with its Roman statues and columns reflected in ornate mirrors alternated with opulent oil paintings. After the down-to-earth barbecue places of Kade's hometown, the place was spectacular, and the scent of freshly made, right-out-of-the-oven bread added a soft touch.

Clean-shaven in a tailored gray suit and shiny leather shoes, the guy was a picture of a successful man. Though his hair—Kade's same tawny shade—had clearly come from a bottle, his hairline showed no hint of receding. Few wrinkles etched his face, likely due to plastic surgery.

When he'd asked his biological father if he'd had any regrets, wishing to hear how sorry he'd been for abandoning his child, the man had poured himself more wine.

Of course, he had.

He regretted being caught, but he'd do better the next time.

Much better. He'd learned new skills, discovered a new talent.

He'd leaned closer and whispered, a smug smile on a face that so eerily resembled Kade's. "I became a con artist, an emphasis on artist. And unlike *conventional* art"—he'd gestured to the paintings—"it pays very well."

He'd been doing it for years now, and nobody was the wiser.

After all, he'd been doing what he was born to do. It wasn't his fault that marks could be so gullible.

He'd teach Kade all he knew, too.

Kade, after being close to choking on his pasta and sea scallops, had refused.

Had he regretted leaving his son to foster care?

The question had burned through Kade in quiet moments all his life, something inside him aching to know how heart-wrenching abandoning him must have been, and finally, he had the chance to ask it.

The guy's eyes widened.

He had no other choice. It had been for Kade's good. It wasn't like he could raise a kid in prison. And Kade had turned out well, hadn't he?

To think about it—the guy had winked as he raised the glass to toast their meeting—he'd done Kade a favor.

His heart heavy, Kade leaned against his bedroom wall as more memories assailed him.

"Do you know how my biological mother is doing?" Kade had pushed away his plate then. Though the food had been delicious, he'd lost his appetite.

"We lost touch many years ago. Men like me don't stay with one woman for long." He'd polished off his veal. "Men like *us*. We're in too much demand. Yes, even at my age." He'd shrugged, confidence shining in his eyes. "Besides, so many lonely women will do so much for attention and a sliver of comfort. Not even anything physical. I have more work than I can handle, and I'll be glad to share."

Nausea rose inside Kade.

"You don't want to face the truth, do you?" Kade had asked at the end of dinner.

"What truth? Truth can be twisted to one's advantage. You'd be surprised how people will give you everything once you keep telling them what they want to hear. In a way"—he'd winked again—"I do them a favor. I give them the happiness they crave, even if only for a little time. For a price, of course. But everything has a price, doesn't it?"

The man had called yesterday and said he'd wanted to see his grandson. A lump formed in Kade's throat.

His hands fisted, and he uncoiled them finger by finger. He couldn't invite his father to the wedding. He couldn't let him near his son or Heather.

What kind of unforgiving son did that make him?

And what kind of *man* did that make him, carrying those genes in his DNA?

He shook his head and returned from his worrisome past to the lovely present lying here.

As he'd expected, Heather had been wearing the puppy-pattern pajamas, buttoned up to the very top, and the sweet sight smoothed his raw insides somewhat.

Her lustrous hair fanned out, a stark contrast to the white pillow, and the rays of sun sneaking through the curtains created lighter streaks in it as if painting subtle highlights.

Her long lashes trembled once, and so did her lips, and he tensed.

Then her lips stretched into a smile, and her breathing evened out again. Unlike her sister's, Heather's lashes were real, as well as her fingernails, and… Well, all about her was real, and he liked it.

He liked it a lot. And her skin, he'd remembered from yesterday, was so smooth to touch that he longed to touch her again.

Hold on.

Wait a minute.

Waaaaait a minute.

Was he attracted to his wife?

He suppressed a chuckle. That wouldn't be so bad if their marriage was based on love for each other instead of love for his child.

Her smile widened, and she whispered something. He leaned closer, desperate to know what in her dreams made her look so happy.

"Oh, Kade…" she whispered again.

He jerked back.

Was *he* in her dreams? And, if so, why did the thought give him such a strong jolt of satisfaction?

But now he felt like an intruder. Besides, as bad as his cooking skills were, she deserved breakfast in bed on her first day as a married woman, and he needed to call to check on Landon.

He tiptoed out and spent the next quarter of an hour enjoying FaceTime with his precious boy.

Then Kade walked to the kitchen and smiled at the puppy drawings on the wall and taped to the fridge. A new drawing depicted humans and a dog. A man, a woman with long brown hair, and a kid near a tree, all standing on green grass.

Their family.

Landon had added her to their family with much more ease than Kade expected, and he wasn't sure whether to be glad or to worry about it. He picked up the puppy-shaped salt and pepper shakers. This was going to be her kitchen now, too, so she could bring the things she liked.

His shoulders hunched, bracing against a guilty jab.

He didn't know what kind of knickknacks she liked, what kind of music, what kind of books. Had never bothered to ask. And he'd usually been attentive to women, had done his best to find out what they'd liked so he could conquer them, give them things they loved, tell them things they wanted to hear.

He thumped the pepper shaker back on the counter as he recalled the conversation with his biological father.

Was he more like his father than he'd realized?

His hunched shoulders stiffened as a mountain seemed to settle on them, but as his gaze drifted to his son's most recent drawing, that mountain became lighter.

His sister Liberty, who'd continued their adoptive family's legacy and become a veterinarian, once told him that, by instinct, sick animals could often find a plant that would cure them. That, from a thousand plants, they would choose the one they needed.

Had God led him to what he'd needed?

It was ridiculous, but maybe Heather and her honest, solid goodness was exactly what he needed to anchor him in the things about him that were right and true.

Lord, please help me figure this out. Please help me avoid hurting her in the process.

Okay, breakfast.

But coffee first.

He opened the coffeemaker and stared at the filter already in place, packed with coffee. Sure enough, water already filled it, too. He turned it on, and as the invigorating aroma spread through the room, he looked at the kitchen differently.

The coffee cans showed his favorite brand just as cereal containers displayed his son's favorites. A green centerpiece bowl boasted the red apples they both loved—like father, like son. He took a bite, savoring the sweet and tangy taste.

She'd always made sure the kitchen had fresh apples and other things he and his boy enjoyed. His heart shifted. As soon as he'd started making enough, he'd hired the maid and cook who'd worked for his family for decades.

But Heather had never been for hire, despite their arguing at the end of every month and her sometimes reluctantly taking pay for babysitting. Between that and his new feelings for her, a guy could get confused.

His eyes had suddenly opened to just how much Heather had done to improve his life, and how little he'd noticed or appreciated it. He had an idea how to start. But first, he needed valuable information, and he knew exactly who to call.

He pulled his phone out of his jeans back pocket and found his sister on speed dial.

He'd always felt a tighter bond with Liberty, maybe because they were the youngest or maybe because they weren't blood-related to the family, even if she didn't know about her being adopted as a baby.

Or maybe because he'd sensed the same free spirit.

And to think, he'd been jealous of her as a teen, envious of the attention and pampering she'd received as the youngest member. But something about Liberty had always made it difficult to be resentful of her.

"You woke me up. This *betterrrr be gooddd*." Her sleepy voice slurred.

He smiled as he poured himself coffee, the familiar aroma—and the fact Heather had cared to set it up for him even while tired—feeding a hunger he didn't realize he had. "Good morning to you, too, sis. I think I'm a new man after my wedding night."

A groan traveled down the line. "Please, spare me the details!"

He chuckled and finished the apple. "That's not what I meant. I just started seeing things I haven't seen before. You're right. I might be a moron who doesn't know what's good for me."

This was her time to chuckle. "Glad to help."

"Speaking of help. I need to know what kind of pastries Heather likes."

"Huh. Okay, take a pen and write this down. Heather never met a pastry she didn't like."

He laughed. "That simple?"

"Some things, my darling brother, are that simple. Now, looks like you have a job to do. And I need to get some sleep. You owe me that much. After wearing a dress at *your* wedding, I stayed up all night with one of *your* horses."

"What horse? What's his or her name? It's not Spirit, is it? Is he okay? Why didn't anybody call me?" He stood up straighter, every muscle tautening.

"It was Inkblot, and she's perfectly fine now. Honest. If I told you, your wedding night would be totally different. Bye, a new man."

After some thinking, looking through recipes on his phone, making sure with his brother that *all* the horses were okay, and soul searching, Kade settled for a delivery from a restaurant and a pastry shop with instructions not to ring the bell but send him a text when the delivery arrived.

As Mac, one of his brothers, insensitively pointed out, it wouldn't do to give his newlywed wife indigestion on her first day of marriage.

Once the deliveries arrived, Kade arranged everything on a tray and added a glass holding a single white rose. The fragrance reminded him of Heather, and his lips stretched wider.

At her soft footfalls in the hall, he looked up.

She appeared in the kitchen, her hair messy, but cuter than her usual braid wrapped on her nape. She'd changed into baggy gray pants and a plain white T-shirt that seemed a size too big, as usual, and he missed her fun pajamas.

Huh.

He missed the simple but charming white long-sleeved gown she wore yesterday, too. With flowers in her hair and that gown skimming her calves, she reminded him of a nymph. When he'd been little, his birth father had read him a book about nymphs living in a brook, and Kade had dreamed that one day a nymph would arrive.

Yesterday, finally, she had.

Why did she insist on wearing baggy clothes as if she were trying to hide inside them? The same way she hid behind her long bangs and thick glasses?

Her mouth formed a silent *O*. She blinked, closed her mouth. "You cooked all that?"

Was she surprised or scared?

"No. But I ordered it. I hope it counts."

She heaved what could only be a sigh of relief. "Totally."

Kade made a promise to thank his brother later. "I wanted to bring you breakfast in bed."

"Really?" She gawked at him. "I mean, wow. I mean, that's so thoughtful of you. But you don't have to do any of this. I know the marriage was for Landon's sake. Pretty much a business deal."

Business deal.

That was all it was to her.

His heart sank a little.

What if at some point he didn't want it to be a business deal?

Well, he'd be wise to remember what she'd said. After all, if he didn't walk away from people in his life, they walked away from him sooner or later.

"I'm sorry I fell asleep in the wrong bed." An adorable blush pinked her cheeks.

"It's okay. I didn't mind." He stepped to her, enjoying her flowery perfume more than he should, letting it remind him of carrying her in his arms yesterday.

While the effort had been... strenuous, it had also caused a pleasant tenderness—such as he'd never felt for anyone but his son—to envelop his body.

Something fragile and gentle encased his heart... as if he had to be careful not to break it.

"My darling wife, we might be an unusual family, but we're a family now. And this is what husbands do for their wives. If they don't, they should. Besides, you took care of my kid for years. It's time I started doing things for you in return."

He was close enough to see tiny dots in her blue eyes, the way her lovely lips parted. Something sweet and vulnerable about her drew him to her more than he'd ever expected.

The pull to take her into his arms, to feel her smooth skin under his fingertips, and to have that pleasant tenderness run through his body again was so strong he almost stepped back to stop himself.

"*Our* kid, please," she whispered. "I'd be glad to adopt him. You know that."

Gratitude spread through him. While the child's mother had

abandoned the boy, while Kade's mother had done the same, Heather was eager to raise a child who wasn't hers. "I know. And I thank you for that."

A shy smile curved her lips. "You know what? Let's eat first, and then you can bring me dessert in bed. The best of both worlds."

He grinned. "Good idea."

After munching on bacon, scrambled eggs, and hash browns, she helped load the dishes in the dishwasher, then disappeared into the hall. He waited a few minutes before he carried the tray to her room.

"Oh, you shouldn't have!" She clapped as if she saw the tray for the first time. A small table already covered her lap.

He placed the tray on the table. "Enjoy."

His thoughts traveled far from the pastries. The urge to touch her became almost unbearable.

Ridiculous. Ridiculous. Ridiculous.

He couldn't understand this urge.

Didn't want it.

He did his best to distract himself with a slice of pecan pie.

She chose an éclair. After biting off a piece, she closed her eyes, and the dreamy smile on her face did strange things to his heartbeat.

"It's sweet and soft and oh so deliciously tender inside," she said with her eyes still closed.

He helped himself to an éclair, as well. "Reminds me of you."

Oops!

Pastry clogged his throat, and he snatched the second water glass, slugging down a few sips.

Her eyelids popped open. "Excuse me?"

"I don't know where that thought came from, but that's true." Maybe he'd be safer with the pecan pie, so he finished it in no time.

She eyed the slice of red velvet cake. "I shouldn't."

"Yes, you should. Do you want me to cut a smaller piece? Tell me how big." He cut a slice much smaller than he'd wanted, but he'd followed her directions.

She scooped a few spoonfuls and closed her eyes again. "Mmm. This is so good."

"No kidding," he muttered, and he wasn't talking about the food.

After she opened her eyes and finished the slice, he leaned to her. "You have some frosting on your face."

"Oh. Here?" She swiped at her face but wasn't anywhere near the frosting.

"Let me help you." He scooped up the frosting with his thumb.

Her eyes widened, and she gasped.

Excitement surged through his veins.

Hmm, marriage could be more fun than he'd thought.

He leaned even closer.

Chapter Seven

KADE'S PULSE GATHERED SPEED. "Our feeding each other tiny pieces of wedding cake from spoons was too prim and proper for me. I think that was totally wrong."

Twinkles appeared in her eyes, and he loved it. "It was more comfortable for me, and thank you for going with it. But maybe we can correct it now and make it more your way." She picked up a wedge of cherry cheesecake with a napkin and brought it to his mouth.

After he ate a few bites, she smashed the rest into his face, laughing. Heather had a fun side to her.

Who'd think?

Then she surprised him even more as she swiped the cheesecake and cherry glazing from his face and licked her fingers. "Delicious indeed."

Delight rushed through him. "Oh, just wait for my revenge!" He took the rest of the velvet cake slice.

"You're not going to do it." She moved the table aside, leaped out of bed, and ran, laughing.

"Watch me." He dashed after her and caught her in his arms, careful not to make her wear the cake.

64

Then he froze, shocked by the way his heart was jumping.

What was happening to him?

This was the same Heather he'd known for years. He'd been accustomed to her presence and had never given her much thought.

How come she made his heart beat so fast now?

Yes, they were married, but it was a pretend marriage.

Wasn't it?

"You caught me. I guess you can feed me the cake now." A playful smile parted her lips.

Was Heather flirting?

That was a first.

He couldn't help smiling in return, but his smile tugged at his heart, sadness weighing its edges. He had her hand in marriage, but he didn't have her heart. And, for some reason, it seemed important now.

Reluctantly, he released her. Then his jaw slackened as she reached to touch his cheek. "What are you doing?"

"I missed some cheesecake." She fluttered her eyelashes in innocence as she brought her fingers to her mouth.

He stifled a groan and placed the cake on the tray. He knew how to play these kinds of games, enjoyed them, maybe even *invented* some of them. But strangely enough, he felt out of his league.

He needed a distraction—and fast—before he lost his self-control.

His gaze fell on the world map. "I know you didn't want to go for a honeymoon now. But one of these days, I'd love to take you on a trip. We can take Landon with us."

Her eyes went big. "I–I don't know. I've never been outside Missouri, and the only time I left my hometown was to go college in St. Louis. How could I even choose?"

"You know how I chose the last few times?"

"No." She shrugged as she studied the map. "I guess you

looked up places online. Did research. Asked friends for recommendations."

That was surely what she'd do.

He chuckled as he picked up a dart from the side table. "I use a much simpler method." He threw the dart, and it landed in Kansas.

She shook her head. "You must be kidding me. That's beyond spontaneous."

"Do you want to try it?" He handed her another dart. "Pick where we're going to honeymoon. Or just the next vacation."

"No, this is…" She hesitated, then accepted the dart from his hands. "I mean… Well, okay."

She stepped back, aimed, and…

"Huh." After moving the nightstand away from the wall, he scooped up the dart from the floor, then repositioned the nightstand. "I guess we're spending the honeymoon behind the nightstand."

She spread her hands. "Oops."

"Well, we can still make it work. I'll move the nightstand away from the wall again. I'll bring snacks and cocoa. We can watch a romantic comedy on the phone and…"

"Um, as *romantic* as that sounds, let me try again." She extended her hand for the dart.

He eyed her. "I should've mentioned that I'm pretty good at this."

The corners of her lips curved up. "Then why don't we do it together? If we're going to spend the hypothetical vacation together, then we need to choose the place for it together, too, right?"

She had a point, though he didn't think of that vacation as *hypothetical*. "Sure. Let's do it."

He gave her the dart, then stepped behind her and faced the map as his fingers circled hers. His treacherous heart started thumping again, and he almost feared she could hear it.

There was something so trusting and reassuring about having her close to him, her hand in his, that filled him with unexpected tenderness.

He drew her hand back, aimed, and…

"Coastal Texas." She nodded, excitement lifting her voice. "Somewhere close to the ocean. Great! That's where I'd want to be. Liberty told me how beautiful it is down there."

Before his marriage, Kade had wanderlust and moved to different states, even backpacked through Europe. He'd spent some time in California during his marriage.

But after the divorce, he'd been stuck in Cowboy Crossing, for Landon's sake. He'd always thought it was temporary, until the boy grew bigger, until the endless horizon with luscious rolling hills and the place where time was slow and horses were fast had grown on him.

As Heather's hand still rested in his, a sense of new wonder filled him.

At that moment, he was right where he wanted to be, too.

She eased out of his embrace as if unaware of the effect she had on him. "I know you like outdoors and sports, and I'm not much for jogging or riding. But maybe we could compromise? Could we go for a walk on one of those trails you talked about instead of a jog?"

"Sounds great to me." He liked her way to find solutions.

When he gave up on things too easily, she worked to solve an issue. Another thing he'd never paid much attention to before.

How many more things was he going to discover? He hoped a lot, and he was going to enjoy every single one.

About half an hour later, they were at the trail. As the wind played with the hair she'd left streaming looose over her shoulders, he ended up looking more at her than around.

When he did look around, a splash of wildflowers along the

path drew his attention, and he picked up a little blue flower, then handed it to her. "The flowers you had in your hair at the wedding were beautiful."

"Shining blue stars. Amsonia illustris. They are my favorite flowers, besides white roses. They bloom in May, so I'm surprised we found them now. I love their shape, like stars." She smiled and tucked the flower in her hair. "Like that?"

"Yes." He stopped and stared, breathing in the flower's fragrance mixed with her perfume.

A shining blue star.

How fitting.

"Thank you." Her smile blossomed, and something inside him did, too.

From afar, the flower was small and unpretentious.

But up close, he could see how pretty it was—a true star. "I'd been on this trail so many times before, but never noticed the beauty of wildflowers or their fragrance. At the ranch, plants just mean a source for hay production."

"Right." Sadness dimmed her eyes.

He cleared his throat. That didn't sound right. "I mean, people put a lot of effort to grow roses and have them bloom. But look at these wonderful creations of God. Nobody sows or waters or nourishes them. Still, they bloom, provide nectar to bees, and bring joy to people."

Something unreadable flashed in her eyes. "Well, people do grow shining blue stars sometimes. But you're right, people pay much more attention to roses." Her voice tightened. "I know it very well."

It must've been difficult growing up with the sister like hers, always being in the shadow of that dazzling beauty and outgoing personality. He drew in a deep breath.

He'd been one such person. But not any longer. Heather might be the one wearing glasses, but he'd been the one nearsighted all these years. "Not all of them."

His heart skipping a beat, he stepped closer. "Heather, I don't know how to say this…"

He meant it. He had no clue how to say that, after years of taking her for granted, he started noticing her.

Okay, maybe that wouldn't sound too flattering. For a person who'd prided himself on always having the right compliment at the right time, why was he scrambling for words now—when he needed them most?

"Say what?" She wrinkled her cute nose in that habit of hers he suddenly found endearing.

Despite her sort of flirting earlier, he knew her well enough to know she wouldn't be playing games. He wasn't going to play games, either.

What he was feeling toward her already, that unexpected spark of attraction, curiosity, surprise, and the shocking urge to taste her pink lips, lovely without any lipstick…

All of that was real.

Or was it because she'd turned away yesterday, hadn't allowed him to kiss her at the wedding, and one always wanted what one couldn't have?

No, it had to be deeper than that.

He tucked a strand of hair behind her ear, causing her to do that gasp of hers that created a whirlwind inside him. "You don't give yourself enough credit. You don't see yourself the way God does."

She chuckled without mirth but at least didn't pull away. "C'mon. I was missing when God gave out beauty, and it all went to my sister. I can see myself in the mirror."

"Then you're looking at yourself through the wrong glasses. The same wrong glasses I used to look at you through." Okay, maybe that didn't sound right.

Heather stooped and picked up another flower, a wilted one

someone had stomped on. "Sometimes people hurt these little flowers, even if unintentionally."

He understood what she was saying, and that had been his biggest hesitation in marrying her. But a small part of him whispered that, if they went their separate ways eventually, he wasn't sure whose heart would end up broken.

"Once someone takes time to look closer, you're pretty like that flower. Very much so."

Instead of smiling like he'd expected, she drew back. "Don't. Just don't. Rumor is you've made giving compliments into an art form. But please don't say things you don't mean."

He stepped toward her.

Okay, maybe he didn't have the best of reputations, but how could he persuade her he deserved the benefit of the doubt? "I meant it. Every word. And I really, really mean what I'm about to do now."

He tipped her face with his thumb, eliciting a sigh, and looked in her eyes, searching for the answer. Her breathing went shallow, and her eyes widened again, longing and something else he couldn't decipher yet in her deep blue orbs.

His heart jumped into his throat.

Then she stepped aside, and his heart sank.

"I know you don't give a kiss much significance. But *I* only kiss someone when I mean it." She walked forward.

He kept up with her, mixed emotions teasing him. Had she just taught him a lesson? Or was she simply not ready? "Then your kiss is truly a gift."

"More like a promise."

They walked in silence until she gestured to a wooden bench. "Could we sit down, please?"

"Sure." He took a seat by her side.

She traced the surface near her with her fingertips. "*B* plus *M* equals heart. Nobody ever wrote things like that for me."

He pulled a penknife from his pocket. "No problem."

As he carved their initials and heart on the bench, the words sank in. Despite being juvenile, the gesture felt like a promise, too.

He scooted closer and traced the outline of her face, staring into incredible *shining blue stars* he'd never noticed before. She stilled.

Then joy, like a falling star, shot through him as she leaned into his touch.

At the footfalls of little feet and a loud "Uncle Kade!" Heather jolted back as if they were teenagers caught kissing.

His niece bumped into his legs and hugged them, and he recovered fast enough to rise and lift her up. He did his best to hide his disappointment. This was a public place, after all, and he loved the girl dearly.

Danica gave out a delighted squeal.

Mac had a look of discomfort as he walked to them. Kade probably wasn't concealing his feelings about their interruption as well as he hoped.

He could usually tell by the tightness of his brother's jaw if he had a bad day at work, or if Danica, who had difficulty fitting in at the daycare, hadn't had such a great day, either.

Mac had never complained, never even badmouthed his wife, but over the years, Kade had learned by that little tightness of his jaw when something had been wrong.

No such thing today.

Kade's thoughts turned again to the darling boy so easy to take care of, his love, his treasure, his buddy. He sent up a prayer of gratitude for his blessings.

The boy was a fun, sociable, agreeable kid for the most part. He was popular in daycare, and neighbors loved having him for a playdate with their kids, especially considering they'd get playdates at his house in return where there were loads of toys and yummy food. Kade had a great babysitter from the time he'd returned to Cowboy Crossing.

Unlike Mac, who'd had to go through separating a babysitter from a chair his daughter had glued her to and getting another babysitter down from a tree. That little girl had made adults and kids alike cry in daycare. Mac had taken his daughter to numerous sessions with a child psychologist, but nothing seemed to help.

Mac was a mountain of a man, six feet tall, with shoulders as wide as the sky above them, and like the mountains, he'd never—okay, almost never—showed emotions. But the family knew how much he hurt inside.

Quiet, hardworking, responsible, he'd been what the family had needed, what this land had needed when their father died. Mac was twenty-one then, and Kade eighteen, both heartbroken.

After a few months at the family ranch, Kade couldn't see the place without the man he'd grown to respect and love, couldn't stand it knowing another person he'd cared about had abandoned him. He'd left for the Texas oil rigs, the first job he could find.

His other brother, Maverick, had left to become a car racer, and his older sister had been gone by then already, staying in different European countries and showing up only for the funeral. Liberty was supposed to leave for college the next year on a scholarship but decided not to. Their mother was drowning in grief at first.

The family was falling apart, and the ranch was struggling, with much of it sold in parcels already.

Mac had dropped out of the university when he'd been close to getting his degree in agriculture, helped their mother, sent Liberty off to college, took over the struggling business, and expanded it. Okay, Maverick winning prizes and donating them to the ranch had helped, too. And their mother, when recovered from grief, had done a great job.

But it had been mainly due to Mac's work and dedication they all still had this legacy.

Guilt needling him at how much he owed his brother, Kade winced.

"Sorry, bro," Mac mouthed to him. Out loud, he said, "Hi, Kade. Hello, Heather."

Maybe Kade should talk to his brother.

Partly because of being the oldest, partly by nature, Mac was a responsible type, a man of few words, but those words were wise.

Maybe because Mac resembled his father so much, the same dark beard, the same height, the same quiet demeanor, and the same hardworking ethics and love for the land and animals, Kade had always imagined his eldest sibling having the kind of marriage his adoptive parents had. Solid, with mutual love and respect—one that would last a lifetime.

Unlike Kade's, Mac's wife wasn't a superficial beauty who didn't want to stick to one place or one man for long. No, his wife had left him with a precocious little daughter because she'd succumbed to alcohol addiction.

At least, Kade's heart had been broken only once. Mac had it crushed twice, first by his first love. Then years later this…

Why did such things happen even to the best of men?

Lord, please heal my brother's heart.

"Down." From her perch in his arms, little Danica interrupted his silent prayer.

Kade understood her reasons once he lowered his niece to stand.

"Heather!" She hugged Heather, who leaned down to hug her back.

Heather had babysat for his brother, and Kade had assumed she'd needed the money. After seeing her excellent references, websites, and her large client list, he knew it wasn't so. She could've made much more with her IT skills.

Instead, she'd chosen jobs paying way less. Maybe out of the goodness of her heart, maybe because she loved kids, but most

73

likely both.

As if sensing he wanted to talk to his brother, she wrapped her fingers around the girl's hand and gestured ahead. "Let's see if we can find a rabbit or a squirrel."

"Yeah!" Danica did a fist pump and giggled.

As the females walked away, he sat on the bench and gestured to Mac to join him. "I need to talk to you."

Mac frowned as he claimed an empty spot. "Okay, I didn't want to believe this. I know you've had a lot of one-day relationships, if one can call them relationships. But you can't get out of marriage after only two days. A day and a half, really. She's a wonderful woman. She doesn't deserve to be left like that. You need to put an effort—"

"Hold on." Kade lifted his hand. "I don't want to get out of my marriage. It's the opposite. I need to learn how to make it last."

A squeal made him smile.

Probably the girls saw a squirrel.

His brother grinned. As he was a serious type, his smile made a rare—and now a surprising appearance—on his face. "Yes! And I'm not saying that because I have my own interest in this."

Uh-oh.

Kade frowned as he took a deep breath of grass-and-wildflower-scented air. "What kind of interest?"

"Oh." Mac looked away as if he said too much. Then he looked him straight in the eye. "Well, you're going to find out sooner or later. See, there's a bet around town on how long your marriage is going to last this time."

Kade grimaced. That was so not what he needed. Hopefully, Heather wouldn't find out about this bet. "Okay, so how much time are folks giving us?"

"I want to say first that people in this town do love you. Very much."

Great. Just great.

He groaned and drew a full chest of fresh air again. "What, like a month? A year?"

Based on another squeal, the girls scared a squirrel or a rabbit again.

"A few gave it a day."

That solicited another groan. "Seriously? I'm surprised you made a bet, knowing you're not the betting kind."

His brother shook his head. "I'm not. I didn't actually lay down money. I just wanted to say my piece to the guys about the bets. But I know you well, and I believe in this marriage. Yep, you and Heather are total opposites, but... Weird as it sounds, it's like God made you for each other. I prayed hard about this before voting for you to marry her. And I've prayed a lot again after the wedding. I believe I'm getting the same answer."

That confidence made Kade breathe easier. "Well, so I guess you didn't just give us a year or two."

"No. If you don't mess up too much, I'm sure you'll stay married for life."

CHAPTER EIGHT

THE NEXT DAY, Heather smiled as she brushed Dara's long hair in the spacious backyard with Landon helping her. "Stay still, please. Stay!"

The boy wasn't exactly helping by trying to pet the dog and distracting her. Heather attempted a frown and repeated more firmly, "Stay still, please."

"Auntie H, she doesn't listen to you." Landon started running circles around them, which caused Dara to move her head to follow his movements, then attempt to get up when she wanted to follow him, period.

"Landon, I was talking to you. If you stayed in one place, that would be helpful. We can play Frisbee after I'm done here." Her frown didn't last as she pressed on the dog's back in an attempt to have her remain in place.

She couldn't be upset at either the boy or the pet, and they knew it.

"Frisbee! Yay!" The child stopped in his tracks.

Based on the dog's joyful bark, she liked the idea, too.

Would Kade like the idea when he got home?

Her heart made a strange movement. Pretend marriage or not,

waiting for a husband to come home created some wonderfully weird palpitations, something she'd never experienced.

Then she'd never been married before, either.

Married to Kade.

The words produced a sweet taste, like the red velvet cake he'd fed her yesterday. And when he'd touched her face, getting the frosting… She closed her eyes in pure bliss.

Whoa.

Now she was the one getting distracted.

She opened her eyes and managed a few more brushes as she listened to the birds, barely able to believe this was all a reality.

Despite being adopted into a wealthy family, Kade hadn't taken a dime from them after giving nearly everything to his ex in the divorce. Her sister had told her about fleecing him for all he was worth because "all that stupid man wanted was his son."

Hurt for Kade and his boy squeezed Heather's heart. Josephine even bragged about how she didn't want to keep Landon in the first place and still duped Kade into relinquishing it all to her. The precious little boy wasn't a bargaining tool. He was a treasure, but Josephine had never understood that.

After returning from California to Cowboy Crossing, Kade had worked hard and saved enough to add an equestrian ranch and buy a fixer-upper house, with Landon's stamp of approval.

She'd driven past this place before he'd bought it, and what a difference!

With help from Mac, he'd built the white picket fence contrasting the emerald-green grass. Then he'd redone the gray-shingled roof and built a wraparound porch and even painted the exterior a macaroni-and-cheese orange—Landon's favorite color.

He'd bought a trampoline and constructed a fern-green treehouse on the largest oak with a slide unrolling from its happy face like a tongue lapping up the dewy lawn and, of course, a doghouse for Dara. A swing dangled beside it.

If Landon was a girl instead of a boy, Kade would surely have built a castle-shaped dollhouse there, too.

Admiration warmed her as she made a few more strokes of the brush while keeping an eye on Landon.

Before, the house had looked gloomy and run-down, with windows broken, shingles missing, and paint so faded and peeled one couldn't say what color it was. It looked bright and cheerful now.

Could her broken heart be changed the same way, by the same man? She shook her head to her thoughts. Her heart wasn't a fixer-upper.

"Landon, I'm almost done," she called out to her son, now playing on the slide.

Her son.

Another new word that tasted oh so sweet on her tongue. He didn't call her "Mommy" yet, and she hadn't officially adopted him yet. But it didn't matter. What mattered was that the boy loved her.

Unlike his father.

She stifled the unwelcome thought and swept dog hair into a dustpan, then threw the hair away and washed her hands in the nearby faucet.

Why pine for things that couldn't be? She should store these small pieces of happiness while she could.

Landon, by that time, scrambled into the swing. "Can you push me, please?"

"Sure." She walked over and pushed his swing, delighted by his laugh.

He looked so much like Kade already….

"Make it stop!"

As the child's demand chilled her heart, she did her best to stop the swing as fast as she could. "What happened? Did you get scared?"

"No. Daddy is home!" The boy leaped from the swing and ran to the patio doors, followed by Dara.

Her heart skipped a beat as Kade entered the yard, lifted his son in the air, then placed him on his feet, and leaned to pet Dara.

How…

What…

How should she behave?

She should welcome him home, of course, and a jolt of joy thrilled her over seeing him. She wanted to kiss him, hug him, make sure this all wasn't a dream, but reality.

As warmth tingled through her, she winced from a pang to her heart. Real wives could kiss their husbands. That wasn't her.

That marriage of convenience was a crazy, crazy, craaaaaazy idea. She should've never done it.

"We cut Dara's hair. Doesn't she look good now?" Landon's face lit up.

As Dara pranced around, chasing her tail, as if to show off her new haircut, Heather smiled at the word *we*, still rooted to her place.

"She sure does." Grinning at her, Kade appeared to guess who'd done the job. "We, huh?"

"Yeah." With a nod, Landon ran his tiny fingers over the smooth fur. "We're a team now, right?"

Something flashed in Kade's eyes. Then his lips widened even more. "Right. A team and a family. You all did a wonderful job, buddy."

A team and a family.

As if it were real.

Her throat constricted, and breathing became difficult. As happy tears watered her eyes, she couldn't prevent them from spilling.

She blinked fast. How silly to cry from something like this.

"Why are you crying? You sad? Did I say wrong?" Landon's

lower lip trembled.

"No, darling. I'm happy." She ruffled his soft hair, overflowing emotion escaping her eyes.

With his thumb, Kade wiped a tear running down her cheek. "And I'm happy for you and happy to be home. I believe we have something to celebrate. I'll get the barbecue going."

"I… We…" She searched for words to express how she felt, but couldn't find any.

"I know." He brought her close, kissed her cheek, and hugged her in earnest.

Who'd think that, of all people, Kade would understand her without words?

But then, she was finding out there was more behind the careless womanizer bravado of his youth.

Much more.

She finally remembered what she was supposed to say. "Welcome home."

He chuckled against her ear. "And what a great welcome it is."

She melted in his embrace like ice cream in the sun. "I missed you."

Uh-oh.

She swallowed hard. Maybe she shouldn't have let that slip. And really, he was only gone for one day of work. He'd been gone from Cowboy Crossing for years before, and she'd missed Landon then while she hadn't missed Kade at all.

He let her go—too soon for her liking—and looked in her eyes, his gaze inquisitive. "You did? Good to hear, because I missed you, too. All of you."

Her insides turned to mush, but her analytical skills took over. Okay, she could believe he missed his son and his dog, but that he missed her?

Hmm, his gaze was sincere. She needed to look away but couldn't force herself to do it. She could get lost in those dark eyes…

"Dad, um, barbecue?" Landon's voice jerked her out of her mental fog.

Dara supported him with her bark, probably hoping there'd be some delicious food for her, too.

Heather drew a deep breath of fresh air. A lot of females in Cowboy Crossing had lost themselves in Kade's eyes, after all, and it didn't end well for any of them. But right now, as he hugged her when they walked into the house and smiled at her, she didn't want to remember that.

Not at all.

"Wash your hands, please. I've made some cheese sticks and turkey and cheese sandwiches, to hold us over before the barbecue." Landon loved all things cheesy.

Like she did, if she was such a sucker for Kade's compliments.

Squaring her shoulders and deciding to resist his charm, she marched to the kitchen. Kade had called her at lunch to see how she was doing and suggested the barbecue, so she'd fed Landon lunch and later took out meat for defrosting.

A sense of wonder awed her as they sat at the table and shared snacks and a large pitcher of her special lemonade.

She'd eaten with him before, but then she'd been just a babysitter.

This meal with all of them as a *family* created such an overwhelming sense of wonder that she was afraid to let go if she breathed too deeply or made sudden movements. And getting to know this new, caring Kade contributed to that somewhat.

Okay.

She munched on the gooey deliciousness.

It had contributed to it *a lot*.

"Nobody took care of me like that," she blurted out.

"Even your parents?" Kade's eyebrows shot up as he refilled

her glass, then Landon's.

"Dad cooked dinners for us when he had time, yes, but I had to do a lot of chores from a young age." Her stomach clenched.

She didn't mean to complain. She'd accepted that her sister, the beautiful and outspoken one, had to be pampered to grow up into a beauty queen or a famous actress and take them all out of poverty.

Nobody pinned any hopes on plump, introverted Heather, not even her father.

"That wasn't fair. Your sister had to do none of the chores?"

"How did you guess?" She placed another serving on Landon's now-empty plate, then sipped her cold drink.

Kade shrugged as he drained his lemonade glass. "I guess something about her insisting on always getting takeout and having a maid gave it away."

He must've guessed the topic was unpleasant to her because he asked, "Why did you decide to work in IT, become a freelance software developer and a web designer? I've seen your work. It's incredible. And your references are spectacular."

Her heart expanded. Even if he was famous for telling women what they wanted to hear, she wanted to believe he was sincere now.

Because his praise mattered to her.

A lot.

She munched on a sandwich. "Once I realized I was good with computers, it gave me something I craved so much. I could help others by fixing something they didn't understand. Finally, I was needed and appreciated."

As a slow nod dipped his chin, his eyes narrowed. "I can understand that. I never realized how bright you are."

"Well, I don't know about that." She waved off his praise. "What's also important, I was able to connect with people online. Finally, I was someone besides a geek or 'fat lard'."

A muscle twitched in his jaw. "Kids can be very cruel. I'm sorry it happened to you."

"Actually, thanks to your sister and you and your brother letting me sit at your table during lunch, the bullying stopped. I still don't know why she stood up for a poor, chunky, unpopular girl. But I'm so glad she did."

"That's the way my sister is. I wish I'd noticed the bullying and stopped it myself." His voice thickened.

Was that genuine regret? It sure sounded like it.

She still remembered the day the teasing had gotten so bad a guy taller and older than her shoved her to the floor, accompanied by laughter from the others. Heather had wanted to disappear then, become invisible, or even stop existing. Her vision blurred.

Then the chanting about "fat lard" stopped.

Somebody pulled her from the floor.

First, she saw cowboy boots. Then, as she looked up, a flash of emerald-green short hair. Strangely enough, the guy who'd tormented her was on the floor now, holding a hand to his face.

"What's going on here?" Kade's voice traveled down the hall.

"Nothing," the guy answered, and people scattered.

He'd probably hit back, but everyone knew the Clark family stuck together.

"We'd love it if you sat with us at lunch. Right, Kade?" Liberty looked at her brother. He nodded, and when everything came back to focus, Heather had known her life would never be the same. Who knew what would have happened if they'd gone to a bigger school, one where they staggered the lunch breaks?

Liberty and she had become best friends for life, and she'd ended up spending time with her, even overnighting at the mansion where Liberty and her mother still lived. Heather's father had been too tired and overworked to protest, and her mother had never cared.

Heather drained her glass, needing something to flush down

bittersweet memories.

She'd been a guest then, a welcome guest, but never in her wildest dreams had she thought she'd marry into this prosperous family where people truly cared about each other.

About half an hour later, as Landon climbed onto the trampoline and started jumping on it—she was thankful for the net keeping him inside—she walked to the grill. She made sure she still kept an eye on the kid, no matter how much she wanted to stare at Kade.

She breathed in the mixture of grilled meat and his cologne and went dizzy. Or maybe his attentive gaze had to do something with it. "Need any help?"

"Just stand near me and let me look at you." A grin crinkled up his suntanned cheeks. "That would help a lot."

That smile lighting his handsome face and the words lighting her heart turned her insides into mush again. She did her best to steel herself against this effect he had on her.

Failing, she sighed. "You're joking again."

This was his modus operandi. He was this way with all women, wasn't he?

Yet her heart didn't want to listen to her mind.

"I'm serious." He flipped the steak and chicken fillets. "You look… radiant today. And I love your dress."

Her cheeks warmed up.

Who dressed up to cut the dog's hair? Especially considering she rarely wore dresses. "Your mother dragged me to the store kicking and screaming after we chose my wedding dress. She helped me choose this one."

Considering that all Heather's mother's attention had gone to her sister, and her father had no clue how to teach a girl to apply makeup or choose clothes, Heather had to teach herself. Or, rather, avoid learning and just put on baggy pants and oversized T-shirts to hide her extra weight.

Make it simple because nobody paid any attention to her, anyway.

Until now.

Kade paid a lot of attention now. "I'm glad she did. The blue floral pattern matches your eyes, and it just… matches you."

Under the clear admiration in his gaze, her cheeks flamed even more. After all the gorgeous women he'd dated, trying to appeal to him was a tough job. She'd even applied mascara and lipstick.

She'd bought that mascara months ago on a whim, but until her marriage, it was as unused as her sister's conscience.

With an effort, Heather moved her gaze to Landon and waved at him. "Wow. You're bouncing like Tigger!"

"You smell good, too." Kade looked at his son, but spoke to her, then leaned closer and kissed her cheek.

Her heart somersaulted.

Men shouldn't kiss a woman unless they meant it. Especially men as handsome as Kade. That just wasn't right. There should be a law against it.

She took a deep breath of mouthwatering scent. "It's the steak."

"No, it's you." He laughed. "The steak aroma might've made my stomach grumble, but it never made my head spin."

Could she have *that* effect on him?

Hope, as intangible as a breeze, stirred her while wind ruffled her hair. She'd let her hair fall over her shoulders because he'd seemed to like it.

All these years, she'd felt like a human equivalent of furniture in his house. The type that could take care of his kid and cook dinners but didn't cause him many thoughts.

The type that definitely didn't cause the admiration in his brown eyes now.

Admiration?

For her?

She must be imagining things. "You and your compliments again."

"Look how high I can jump!" Landon yelled from the trampoline.

"You're doing great!" Kade yelled back.

"You really are. But be careful!" she joined in.

"All I say to you is true." Kade's eyes grew serious as his gaze swept to her lips, then moved to her eyes again.

Did he…

Did he want to kiss her?

With the thought, she stood taller. She might not be a raving beauty like her sister, but she could be pretty, too, couldn't she?

She'd been upset with God for making her chunky and unattractive, for having it as the reason she'd grown up unloved by her mother.

Could that self-image of a lonely unloved girl be something she'd created due to hurtful words from her mother, sister, and classmates? Maybe Kade was right and that wasn't what God had meant for her at all.

She was so much more than her extra weight.

So much more.

Kade stepped closer. "I see something in you now that draws me to you. It's like God finally opened my eyes."

Time stood still.

Then her breathing went irrational.

This was what happiness was made of.

It smelled of Kade's intoxicating cologne and delicious steak on the grill. It sounded like the birdsong in the trees and the loud beat of her heart. It looked like the man she was falling for and the child and dog she already loved.

And it felt…

A delightful wave swept her up.

It felt like nothing she'd felt before.

Kade cupped her face, and she needed all her willpower not to raise to her tiptoes and wrap her arms around his neck.

From the corner of her eye, she saw Landon clamber off the trampoline. A kiss meant a promise to her, and she wasn't sure either she or Kade were ready for it yet.

With an effort, she moved away, and he let her go.

"You did great." She bent to the boy and hugged him, a different wave of tenderness washing over her.

He hugged her back, then wiggled out of her embrace. "I know. Food ready?"

I know.

She chuckled. This boy inherited his father's confidence.

"Just a few more minutes." Kade lowered the fire.

"Okay, I'll go play Frisbee with Dara. We promised her, and we gotta keep a promise." The boy gestured for Dara to follow him, and she obliged.

"Gotta keep a promise. I know all fathers say it, but I'm proud of my son," Kade whispered. "I mean, our son."

Then, much louder, he said, "Landon, please stay where we can see you but far enough from the grill."

"We don't wanna fry the Frisbee. Duh!" The boy ran to the further side of the backyard.

Kade stepped closer, close enough that his breath tickled her skin. "I should've told you something about me and your sister."

Oh no.

No, no, no.

"Yes?" She swallowed hard.

He wasn't going to tell her he still loved her sister, was he?

Please, please, don't. Please!

Days ago, it wouldn't matter as much. Now it mattered the world to her.

"We didn't divorce because she left me. She wanted that to be the official version, one of her conditions for giving me Landon,

87

and I went with it. We divorced because she cheated on me. Twice. The first time, I stayed married to her for Landon's sake." The crinkles whitened around his eyes, and his jaw tightened.

"But the second time, you couldn't." She didn't say it as a question but as a statement. She'd never thought before how divorce must've hurt him.

Rumors around town suggested the divorce was from mutual agreement. Neither he nor her sister wanted to be tied down to one person. Heather had believed the rumor because it suited what she knew of Kade and Josephine's characters.

She knew better now, or at least, she did about Kade. She hoped.

"I couldn't stay. That's not the life I wanted for Landon."

"I wouldn't do that to you. Even though it's not a real marriage."

Emotion gleamed in his eyes. "It's started to feel real to me."

What?

Her eyes widened. Did he just say that?

Could there be hope that the growing attraction wasn't one-sided?

Her phone rang, and she reached for it in her dress pocket, her mind in a daze. Her mouth slackened at Josephine's name on the screen, as if her only sibling could feel them talking about her many miles away.

"It's my sister." And his ex-wife. *Could this situation get any more awkward?* "I have to take this—I'm sorry."

"Hello, sis," she said into the phone, trying to infuse warmth into her voice and only partially succeeding. "If you're calling to ask about Landon, he's doing fine."

"No, that's not why I'm calling." Josephine laughed, the sound a little muffled by the motor's background growl. "I know he's in good hands. I should say I'm sorry I didn't make it to your wedding. But I'm not. Not like you wanted me there, anyway, right?"

A lump formed in Heather's throat as she leaned against the house's wall, its cheery macaroni-and-cheese color mocking her turmoil. "I understand the situation is unusual and is… difficult for all of us. And I'm sorry if it would be painful for you to be here."

"Painful? No. Anyway, here's the reason I'm calling. I broke up with my boyfriend."

"Sorry to hear that. The one who is an actor?" Keeping up with all the boyfriends took a spreadsheet.

"No, that one was before the restaurant owner. And that one was before the producer. Then there was another producer… Anyway, my acting contract is over, and I decided to come back for some time. Maybe spend a few days with my son. You wouldn't mind if I stay at your house, right? It's empty now, and I could use some privacy."

"You're coming back." Gasping, Heather nearly dropped the phone.

Could this get any more awkward?

She just received the answer.

CHAPTER NINE

THE NEXT DAY AFTER DINNER, Kade resisted the urge to gnash his teeth. The evening had gone from wonderful to a disaster in minutes, and he owed it all to his ex.

Well, this had to change.

He couldn't let her keep affecting his life and his family. He'd tried to cheer Heather up yesterday, but she'd gone to her room after they'd tucked Landon in bed, her sad eyes making his heart squeeze.

Her shoulders had been slumped and her look forlorn, like now.

He straightened his back as they cleared the table.

Today had to be different.

As soon as he and Heather placed the last dish into the dishwasher, he reached for her hand, then looked at Landon, playing with building cubes on the rug. Dara was lying on the floor next to him and from time to time nudged the cube she likely thought would best suit the construction.

The warmth from Heather's hand affected Kade more deeply than he'd intended. Something about having her hand in his calmed him as if it were tangible proof he had an intimate connection with someone.

Someone who wouldn't deceive him and/or disappear the next day.

Not with just any someone. With Heather.

He ached to bring sparkle to her blue eyes again, to make those pink lips smile as when she'd seen him yesterday. Or taste them, tentatively, slowly, deepening the kiss and savoring every moment....

His heartbeat increased.

What was he going to say?

Oh yes.

"It's still early. How about we go for a boat ride at the lake?"

"Daddy, yay!" Landon jumped to his feet.

Kade didn't doubt his enthusiastic response. Dara gave him a reproachful look, as if realizing she was going to be left out, and dropped her head on her paws.

He studied Heather, relieved the corners of her lips curved up.

But then, doubt settled in her eyes. "We'd need to rent a boat, and it might be too late in the day."

Spotting a speck of sauce on her cheek, he removed it with a napkin, soliciting a little gasp. Something pleasant spread through him as her breathing went shallow and her lips parted.

He'd never get tired of that reaction of hers. "Mac has a house at the lake with a dock and two boats, one motorized and one, well, not."

"Oh. Okay. And he lets you use them?" A small birthmark tinted her cheek, close to her jawline.

He'd never wanted to kiss a birthmark this badly in his life.

Concentrate!

"Sure." He shrugged. "Maverick has a villa in Italy, and we all are welcome to use it anytime, too."

Her eyes went big. "Your brother has a villa in Italy?"

"Yup. He won enough car races to afford it. He's invested a

lot in this ranch, too. He says that helps him not feel guilty that he's not here to help in person. We call him a steel cowboy for his love of cars and motorcycles."

Her smile widened. "It fits."

"When the family was deciding where to get a vacation home, he threw a dart, and it ended in Italy. We all like pizza, spaghetti, gelato, and sunshine, so it seemed a good fit." He'd been to Italy while backpacking through Europe, and several images flashed in his imagination.

Him and Landon with Heather in a flowery red dress and a large hat strolling on the beach, her hand in his. Sharing a gelato at one of the plazas with picturesque fountains, the creamy taste even more delicious when accompanied by the joy on her face. Visiting a museum. All of them dining on pizza at a small-town café where it always smelled like cappuccino and the tables were decorated with fresh flowers.

Today, Heather wore her baggy pants again, together with a white T-shirt a size too big. She'd braided her hair and pinned it in a bun.

But now he knew how she looked in a dress that hugged her curves, with her long, luscious hair flowing over her shoulders.

Landon started running circles around Dara. "We're gonna go to the lake! We're gonna go to the lake!"

The dog didn't move, and somehow, he managed not to step on her tail.

Kade's muscles ached a bit after a tiring day at work, but it would hurt much more to see Heather disappear into her room, worried about her sister's upcoming visit.

"What do you say?" He let her hand go, but only to tip her chin with his fingers.

Her eyelashes fluttered. "I say… What are we waiting for?"

"Yay!" Landon stopped running circles, probably to Dara's relief who gave out a sigh. The dog might've worried about her tail, after all. "I'm gonna get my cap."

"Sunglasses, too, please!" Kade called out after his son, who disappeared in the hall.

Years ago, he'd bought matching caps, sunglasses, and T-shirts, because he and Landon were a team. He kept replacing his son's items when the boy needed a bigger size.

"What should I get?" Head tilted slightly to the left, she looked at him.

"Just your beautiful self." He slapped himself on the forehead. "I almost forgot something. I bought you a gift."

"I told you that you didn't have to—"

She was the only person he'd met who didn't want to accept gifts.

He lifted his hand. "I talked to Landon, and he said *we gotta*. You wouldn't object to Landon doing it, right? Wouldn't refuse his gift, I mean, his idea and break his little heart?" He blinked innocently at her.

She chuckled. "That's unfair, to use your son like this."

He touched that enticing birthmark with his fingertips since he couldn't kiss it yet. "Yeah, I'd use Dara, but as smart as she is, she couldn't understand what I was asking her."

As if to confirm this, Dara lifted her head, yawned, and placed her snout on her paws again. Then she closed her eyes.

"You're too charming for your own good. Or, rather, mine." Heather grinned despite her words.

"I hope you'll like it." Apprehension squeezed his heart.

Maybe Heather wasn't the only person who didn't accept gifts. When he'd bought matching clothes for his ex, she'd told him the clothes weren't fashionable enough or expensive enough for her to wear.

At that time, he'd been so smitten he hadn't realized Josephine had also had little interest in being part of the team, part of the family. She'd never wanted to be a mother and had reproached him every chance she'd gotten.

Pushing sad memories away, he rushed to the truck and returned with the packet, grateful he could pick his sister's brain about Heather's size.

A somewhat nervous smile wobbled into place as he handed over the package, a telltale clothing store's label on it. "It's nothing fancy, really, but I hope you'll like it."

"Thank you. Let me try it on." She disappeared in the direction of her room.

He used the time to change into jeans and the matching T-shirt with a Newfoundland puppy who looked just like Dara when she was younger. He put on the gray cap with the same print, sunglasses, and cowboy boots, as well as prepared the fishing rod and other fishing supplies for Landon.

Hmm, this was taking her a long time.

Kade swallowed hard, hoping she didn't change her mind. Then he helped Landon change into a similar T-shirt, life vest over it to be on the safe side, little jeans, and waterproof boots. He packed a blazer for his son, just in case the night cooled.

Still no sign of Heather.

Huh.

His heart squeezed further.

"Daddy, I gonna check on Auntie H." Landon darted to Heather's room.

Moments later, the boy was dragging her out. Well, she was walking of her own volition, of course, because no way a kid of his size could drag an adult. But him tugging on her hand helped.

Then she stopped in the hall. "I don't know how… this looks."

With a sigh, Landon ran around her and started pushing her legs. "You look great. Now can we go?"

Dara must've figured help was needed because she got up, ran to Heather, and nudged her with her nose behind her kneecaps.

Kade did his best to hold in laughter.

"Okay, okay, I'm going." A tentative smile eased the worry from her face.

He grinned. "I second my son. And I didn't know you had jeans like that." Her luscious hair poured over her shoulders again from under the cap, the fun T-shirt with a smiling—yes, smiling!— puppy hugged her, and cowboy boots suited her.

But the best part wasn't what he'd gifted her. Hmm, these were form-fitting blue jeans, unlike the baggy jeans and pants she'd been wearing for years.

"I didn't have them before. Your sister made me buy them." Her smile spread wider.

"I'll make sure to thank her later." He raised a brow. "How exactly could she *make* you buy them?"

"She took them from the rack and shoved me into the dressing room. Apparently, she has much better upper body strength than I do. She stood by the door and didn't let me leave until I promised to buy them and wear them within three days."

This time, he couldn't help laughing. "That sounds like Liberty."

Liberty never had hang-ups about being on the plump side, though her weight often fluctuated. She'd never cared much what people thought about her, period, wearing bright-colored form-fitting clothes if she wanted, emerald-green hair, no makeup or nail polish, with a cowboy buckle among her few accessories. And since she'd started wearing only one earring, like her mother, she'd even created a new trend in town.

"Your sister..." Heather stumbled as if recalling they weren't technically siblings. "I mean, not exactly... Well..."

Liberty, who'd been adopted when she'd been a baby, still had no clue about her adoption. Though several folks in town knew, nobody had revealed it to her, and the family preferred it that way.

After Kade discovered it, he'd wanted to tell Liberty out of spite. He'd been jealous, seeing how much love the family lavished on their youngest.

His stomach did a small roll. He'd been so glad he hadn't. Despite all the love, she wasn't spoiled and had worked on the ranches as much as the guys had while growing up and probably more than they did since she'd gotten her veterinarian degree.

She'd become a goofy tomboy instead of the pampered princess of one of their town's richest families. And she still brightened the day of those around her.

Besides Mac, Kade had grown closest to Liberty. Maybe because Maverick had left soon after high school to pursue a racing career and his older sister had left for Europe even earlier.

However, Liberty had always been part of this land and the small town and loved it with passion.

She'd come up with different projects in Cowboy Crossing, like renovating the library, opening the children's museum, and adding a playground in the park, running fundraisers, and donating a lot herself. She'd been the biggest supporter for his plan to open an equestrian ranch for foster teens.

Admiration and brotherly love warmed him. It had never mattered whether they were blood-related or not. They were soul-related. He couldn't have ached more for a birth sister than he had when Liberty's short-lived marriage imploded.

"She is *my sister*," he said firmly. "And I couldn't wish for a better one."

"What about me, Daddy?" Landon walked to him and tugged at his hand.

That simple gesture would never stop tugging at his heart, too. "I couldn't wish for a better son."

Dara barked, obviously offended.

"Or a better dog." His gaze met Heather's and held. "Or a better wife."

"You didn't choose me to be your wife, remember?" she whispered.

"Well, considering all the choices I've made before, I'm grateful for that. God saw it, and He chose you for me." He planted a quick kiss on her cheek, brushing his lips against that birthmark. His pulse skyrocketed. "Okay, team, time to go."

"Thank you for giving me this gift." Her eyes misted. "For making me feel like I belong in your family."

"Of course, you do. But if I *said* that to you, you'd have told me I'm used to giving compliments. So I wanted to *show* you." And he wanted to keep showing her.

She grinned. "Well, we do live in the Show Me State, don't we?"

"Oh yes."

"Daddy, we're taking Dara, right?" Landon's lower lip stuck out.

Kade bent to him. "No. Remember, she jumped out of the boat last time?"

"But, Daddy, we can't leave her here." The lip stuck out more, tugging at him. "We gotta take her."

He attempted to maintain a stern expression. "Why?"

"Because we gotta." The boy nodded for emphasis.

Huh. "Why?"

"Because we gotta." Three nods this time.

Dara lifted herself on her hind legs, reaching well up to his chest.

His resistance was evaporating, and he turned to Heather. "Help?"

Raising her hands in surrender, she laughed. "Well, *we gotta.* How can we argue with that logic? If Dara jumps into the lake, I promise to jump, too, especially if there are no people around. I happen to be a great swimmer."

Another thing he didn't know about her, something unexpected. It was like a delicious dinner where better dishes came later in the meal. He couldn't wait to see what else was coming.

97

"Dara, promise you'll stay in the boat." Landon stared at the dog.

Dara barked twice.

"Daddy, she promised." His boy grinned at him.

Oh, the precious age when one could believe a dog's promises.

After Kade's sad childhood and disastrous marriage, he wasn't sure he could believe human promises.

His ex's words from this morning's call rang in his ears—*I'm coming back. See you soon, darling.*

He suppressed a grimace.

That promise he could believe.

CHAPTER TEN

MINUTES LATER, with everyone but the dog buckled in his truck, the motor growling in the background, Kade placed a CD in the player. He and Landon often belted out their favorite tunes when they were going somewhere. Dara usually helped by barking.

The country song filled the truck, and he turned on the air conditioner. "Everybody comfortable? Not hot, not cold?"

While Heather nodded, Landon said, "I'm good, Daddy."

Dara barked twice.

Making a turn, Kade stilled.

Hold on.

Did Heather even enjoy country music?

He needed to take her likes and dislikes into consideration. And he couldn't even remember what kind of music she preferred. "Um, what songs do you like?"

"Classical music."

"Oh." How did one belt out to classical music? And he didn't have any CDs with classical music, that's for sure. But he could compromise, couldn't he? "Well, feel free to change to the classical radio station."

"It's okay. I like this, too." She rested her hand over his but removed it far too quickly.

"Daddy, our song!" Landon started yelling the words as the next song started.

He sent her an apologetic glance. "I hope we won't make your ears bleed," he mouthed to her.

Then he joined in.

After a bit, she joined in, too.

They made such a strange chorus, but it felt so right as if it was meant to be. Like God could take discordant notes and somehow still make them fit together.

Some time later, Kade parked near the lake house, and they walked to the private dock. "If everyone agrees, I'd rather take the rowboat. It's more peaceful." And it felt closer to nature.

She hesitated. "Um, sure. I can help row."

While Landon nodded, Dara barked her vote.

Once Kade pushed the boat from the dock, Landon hugged the pet as if to make sure she stayed inside. "You gotta stay. You promised."

The dog wiggled her tail and eyed the water.

Yeah, she'd wait until the middle of the lake to jump, just to make things more difficult. She'd better not capsize them, but if she did, he'd gotten Landon in his life vest.

Considering Kade wasn't a great swimmer, he shouldn't have let his son talk him into taking the dog. Well, too late now.

The lake's mirror surface spread a serene feeling through him, calmed his turmoil after hearing his ex planned to show up and stir things up. He swallowed hard, recalling another thing that clenched his stomach.

His biological father had been more and more insistent on visiting and getting to know his grandson.

Kade frowned as he paddled further but ironed out his frown for his family's sake. There was a reason he'd brought Landon here sometimes, despite having a pond on his property and fishing there, despite being unable to swim well—he was going to learn soon, honest!

Time together with his son here had been a gift.

Just like his mother had said once when he'd been jealous of his little sister after his adoption, Liberty had been a gift for them, too. An unexpected, but a precious gift.

If you treat people well, they might become precious gifts to you instead of being a source of anger.

She was right.

There were exceptions to his rule, like his ex, where no amount of his love and trying to please her made any difference, but exceptions only confirmed the rules.

As the boat glided forward, he stared at the lovely woman wearing the same cap he and his son wore, the same T-shirt.

The wind played with her hair, and he cherished her smile as the scenery obviously had a calming effect on her, too.

"It's gorgeous here." Her lips curved up again.

Moving the oars in a steady motion, he nodded. "I never stop being amazed by the beauty of God's creation."

That smile as she ran her fingers through the water touched something inside him, creating a ripple effect in his heart.

An American avocet with its long beak and peach-colored head and neck swooped across the lake, and she leaned to Landon, pointing at it as if it were something incredible.

It was. They rarely ventured this far north.

Wide-eyed, his boy stared in the sky. "Daddy, did you see it? Did you see it?"

"Yes, I did, buddy."

He finally saw that Heather, the woman he'd taken for granted all these years, could be a gift, too, if he let her.

A gift he didn't ask for, didn't expect, a surprise he'd pretty much rejected when she'd come up with that irritating proposal.

Lord, could this be the woman You meant for me? Or is this someone I'll have to part ways with again?

Without knowing it, just by being there, she reached the part of him he'd thought dead since his divorce.

With the light breeze coming from the lake and white clouds and sun reflecting in peaceful sparkling waters, this was the special place for him and Landon.

Now it could become a special place for Heather, too. Couldn't it?

"I'm glad you like it here."

"I love it." As she tipped her head his way, letting him see under that cap, her face brightened. "I'm usually busy with so many different gadgets that it's been a while since I ventured out like this. Thank you for bringing me."

Why had he?

"Actually, thank you." They neared the middle of the lake, so he slowed.

"For what?" Her eyebrows shot up as she hugged Landon and pointed at another bird, with brown and rusty-brown coloring. "Look, look there!"

"For all you've done for my son and me. But really, for being you. For existing."

He thought she'd refuse the compliment, but her smile just turned more melancholic.

"You do mean it, don't you?" She ran her fingers through the water again, surprise tingeing her voice.

Well, he was as surprised as she was. Why had he considered her plain and unattractive? Maybe because often when she'd talked to him, she'd had that stern expression, as if she were about to scold him, and it rubbed him the wrong way.

Today, she wore different glasses, in a transparent frame, so he could see her blue eyes better. Her smile lit up her face and her eyes, changed it, made it more…open.

Pink lipstick highlighted the plumpness of her lips, and he had to push away thoughts of kissing her.

She made him feel… at ease. Maybe the entire arrangement made him feel at ease, too. He didn't need to win her affection. He could just… be around her.

Just be himself, though at thirty-eight, he still wasn't sure who he was, that he'd found himself. His biological father said there were so many things Kade hadn't tried yet.

"Daddy, are we gonna fish?" Landon interrupted his musings.

Dara, true to her promise, had stayed quiet and didn't even seem to move this time. Go figure.

Kade paddled to turn the boat. "You are. But let's go back toward the shore, okay?"

Though eager to talk to Heather about his biological dad, he didn't want to do it in front of his son. Confusion clouded his mind again. He'd tried to be a good Christian, grant that man forgiveness he'd want for himself. He'd said he'd been on the straight and narrow for years, that he'd tried to change for Kade.

But was it true, or had he just said what Kade had wanted to hear?

The man was a self-confessed con artist, after all.

All kinds of alarms went off in his head when he thought about introducing that guy into Landon's life.

How would it affect the boy when his grandfather up and left one day?

Also, his biological father had asked too many questions about his adoptive family's wealth. Premonition squeezed Kade's heart.

"Look, a school of fish!" Heather pointed somewhere to the right.

"Where?" Kade and his boy said in unison.

The boy leaped to his feet, but Kade nudged him down. The dog remained quiet. She'd earned a treat when they got back.

"Right there. Beneath the surface." Heather gestured to the water.

"I see it. I see it!" Landon clapped.

"Good job, buddy." Kade spotted tiny silvery fish before they disappeared. Then he moved his gaze back to her, the sun highlighting brighter strands in her dark hair again.

That was the thing.

He hadn't looked beneath the surface before, at least not when it came to Heather. But then, he hadn't seen beneath his ex's polished and gorgeous surface at first, either.

To think about it, many first impressions would be wrong. If instead of knowing his eldest sibling for years he'd met Mac soon after his divorce from an alcoholic, he might've written the guy off as a sulking grouch. And as for Liberty—his sister was down-to-earth and told things like they were, including the things Kade didn't want to hear.

Looking beneath the surface wasn't easy, especially inside his own soul or his biological dad's. Kade was too scared of what he might find there.

Once they reached the shore, Landon settled on the dock with a fishing rod and a bait box.

Maybe the boy was getting tired. His usual energy was gone.

Keeping an eye on his kid, Kade arranged two folding chairs from his brother's house close enough to help if anything happened, but far enough to be out of the earshot from curious little ears.

He positioned a cooler in front of the chairs. "Landon, are you doing okay?" he called out. "Want a drink?"

"Quiet, Daddy! Fish gonna hear you and swim away." The boy sent back a reproaching look, then hugged the dog, who kept silent all this time.

That deserved two treats.

Kade gestured to one of the chairs to Heather. "Please take a seat."

He handed her a cool iced tea can. He should've asked her

what drink she wanted first. He'd learn—eventually.

"I need to admit something. Growing up, I envied my sister so much. I envied thin, pretty, rich girls in town who had everything handed to them." Sitting down, she twisted the can between both hands. "Now I think the worst thing you can do to a person is to give him or her everything."

Wow.

Okay, he hadn't expected that.

He breathed in the fresh scent of grass and algae, just a hint of her subtle perfume complementing it.

To think about it, being dumped from one foster family to another, he'd envied kids whose parents hadn't abandoned them. He related to the first part, but not the second.

He snatched a cold, smooth-to-the-touch can for himself and claimed the chair. "Why do you think that?"

"Well, my sister didn't have everything because we weren't rich enough. But from an early age, she knew she only had to smile and pout and she'd get nearly all she wanted. Dad worked two jobs for it, and Mom would get loans that we couldn't afford to repay." She made a pout.

It looked so similar to his ex's expression that he laughed before he realized how serious the matter was.

He popped the can open and sipped the cooling liquid. "That's an interesting theory. I can see how being spoiled and selfish wasn't entirely your sister's fault. But to say the worst thing that can happen to us is to be given everything we wanted…"

"Easy come easy go, as they say. When things come easy to us, we don't learn to appreciate them." She turned her drink can in her hand before taking a gulp. "We take them for granted. We forget to work hard for our dreams."

Watching Landon, who watched the lake and potential fish, Kade reached for her hand and laced his fingers through hers.

Hmm, maybe there was some truth in her words.

Over twenty years ago, he'd found it difficult to believe his adoptive father when he'd told him God put people He loved through trials for a reason.

Kade couldn't see what the reason for trials could be.

Maybe if his first marriage hadn't been so disastrous, constant scenes and arguments, he wouldn't appreciate the peace and quiet of this one. If he hadn't been hungry as a kid, he wouldn't savor the hearty and delicious ranch meals. If he hadn't gone through more than a few uncaring foster families, he wouldn't be so driven to have a vacation ranch for fostered teens.

Still, he would've preferred to avoid those trials.

Winning women's hearts had come so easy to him that after several victories he'd come to take them for granted.

If Heather had dressed and behaved differently when he'd hired her and they had started dating… He probably would've moved on fast, looking for a new girl to conquer, before realizing how amazing Heather was.

He finished his drink and collected the trash. She handed him her empty can.

"Another tea?" he asked her, but she shook her head.

"Daddy, Daddy, I got it!" Excitement palpitated in the boy's screech as he reeled in the fish.

"Hold on. Be careful." Kade rushed to help him.

The last thing he needed was for his kid to fall into the water. As they slid the fish into a blue bucket, Landon beaming at him, tenderness filled Kade's entire being.

And maybe because his parenthood had been so difficult from day one, he'd learned to appreciate every smile on Landon's face, every little hug, and belatedly, all the support Heather had given him.

He'd love Landon just as much, no doubt about it, but he wouldn't have learned so much about himself, wouldn't have grown as much if things had been fine from day one.

"Great job, buddy!" He helped him hook a new worm, then returned to his chair.

Heather waited for him there with a loving smile. "You're so good with him."

"Like he is with me." He settled near her and made sure to have her hand in his again.

His ex had left and returned a few times, and after losing his adoptive father and having his biological one swim in and out of his life at whim, he needed this physical proof that his wife was here to stay.

Hopefully.

"You should take it as a compliment, too. Despite the circumstances, he's a happy, bright, well-adjusted boy." Gentleness filled her eyes.

The same gentleness soothed him. "Well, that's thanks to God sending me you, too. In some ways, it's not just me raising Landon. It's him raising me. I don't know how I'd turn out if God hadn't given me my son. I guess you're right in some ways. I can feel the blessings more after all the difficulties."

They settled in a companionable silence, but then a shadow passed over her face, tightening his gut.

"What are you thinking?" He leaned forward, rubbing his thumb across the back of her hand.

"I... I'm worried." She looked away as if reluctant to continue.

He stayed still.

Should he give her space?

Or ask what worried her?

This marriage-and-relationship thing sure wasn't easy. Fast courtships that barely scratched the surface were so much easier.

Maybe he could guess the source of her worries. "Is it because your sister might come back? Are you worried it'll affect things for you and me?"

107

Still looking down, she nodded. "You loved her once." Her voice was so low he strained to hear it. "Those feelings might come back. And then... what happens to us?"

Chapter Eleven

KADE SHOOK HIS HEAD. "You don't have to worry about that. Not after what happened."

"You can't control what your heart wants."

He shook his head more firmly. "My heart doesn't want her. Not a chance. Not since I met you."

"You met me years ago and never took a second look."

"Now I have. I see the real you, and I can't wait to get to know you more. She changed after marriage. Or maybe once I saw the real Josephine, love ebbed away and never came back. Besides, her beauty, the type that's all on the surface, is fleeting. What you have, that beauty inside, that's forever. It's not going to change or disappear. It's always going to be there, and I find it so very precious."

Her pink lips parted as she gawked at him.

Then she rolled her eyes. "You should be writing manuals 'How to Win a Woman's Heart.' Or do coaching. You're very good at this. Excellent."

Not the reaction he'd been hoping for. "I didn't say an untrue word. Why would I? Your inner beauty shines through when one takes a close look at you."

That bullying in childhood must've gotten to her, multiplied by the mistreatment of her mother and sister. He winced, regretting not stopping it.

His rep didn't help matters, either. He'd been okay with his player reputation, even proud of it.

Not so much now.

He also had a few choice words for her fiancé who'd traded her for her sister before Josephine married Kade. That guy had no clue what he'd lost.

She kept silent a while. "You're right. I'm just insecure." She leaned toward him, squeezed his hand, more tightly locked their fingers together, causing his pulse to hum. "Thank you for being so patient."

"Auntie, Daddy, more fish!" Landon grinned back. The fishing rod stayed unmoving. "Or not."

"You're doing great!" Kade called out, resisting the urge to walk to his son.

A smile stretched her lips so wide little lines crinkled around her eyes. "I don't think I've been this happy in a long time. I'm thankful for every moment."

His heart shifted. "Me, too."

Pleasing her, making her happy, was so easy. It had taken him diamonds and expensive dresses to coax even a hint of a smile from her sister.

Hmm.

If he knew his ex, she often wanted what she couldn't have.

Now when he was married to Heather, she might do everything she could to win him back. Flirting, showing up at his work, spreading rumors in town, trying to kiss him in public, coming to family dinners with an excuse she wanted to see her son, never mind that she'd given him up years ago…

Those would be just a few things she'd do.

It wasn't like he'd go back to that woman—he nearly snorted

at the thought. But Josephine's antics would dim his wife's happiness, and he didn't want that.

While his left hand stayed in hers, he used his right hand to remove a strand of hair that fell on her face, enjoying the smoothness of her skin against his fingertips. "You're like a gentle flower that started blooming, opening petal after petal. How come I knew you for years and never saw how amazing you are until I married you?"

Her face brightened. "Maybe because I didn't start blooming until I married you." She gestured to the lake. "You were like water I needed so badly."

"I guess I married the wrong sister first," he muttered.

No overwhelming passion overtook him in his marriage to Heather like it had initially in his first marriage. But he'd rather have this peaceful joy than a tornado sweeping him up and leaving destruction in its wake.

"Then you wouldn't have had Landon. I do my best to believe trials are given to us for a reason, though as a kid I wouldn't have agreed. For many years, I wanted to be like my sister—beautiful, popular, and confident."

"I'm glad that you're nothing like her." Oops! He caught himself. "Though you're still beautiful."

"At this point, I'm glad, too." She placed her head on his shoulder.

More joy flew through him as he cherished the precious feeling of having her near, so trusting and caring, and the breathtaking view of his little boy and big dog against the sunset.

"These simple moments are what happiness is made of," she whispered.

"I agree."

But thoughts in the back of his mind still made his gut twist.

His ex returning and interfering in his budding relationship with his new wife.

And another one…

He checked on Landon and offered him a drink again—this time quietly—then returned to his chair. "My biological father insists on coming for a visit. He wants to get to know his grandson better and his daughter-in-law."

She studied him. "But you're not sure you want him to."

Man, she was perceptive.

"I'm doing my best to be kind and forgiving. He said so many times that he did what he did for me, so I wouldn't grow up in poverty. I… almost believe him. And I remember good things about him while he still was with us until I was six."

He paused, trying to remember. "Like him flying a kite with me in the park. Buying me ice cream. He tells me about other things I don't remember for some reason, like visiting the zoo. Taking me for a walk. Tucking me into bed and telling a story." Another mirthless chuckle shook his chest. "That one I can believe easily. He tells good stories."

"But there are other memories, too, right?" Her expression gentle, she leaned closer, giving him the whiff of that sweet perfume.

"Yes. Crying myself to sleep and being beaten in foster homes until I learned to toughen up. As for taking me for a walk… I remember him starting a conversation at a park with a woman, and while she aaahed over me, he emptied her purse. He denies that memory, of course."

"I'm sorry," she whispered.

He stared at the lake to let the serenity wash out the resentment, then glanced at his son. "At this point, I don't know which memories are real and which ones he's trying to plant into my head. I don't feel I know the real man who fathered me. Nearly every time he shows up for our meetings, he has a different hair color. Sometimes he wears a beard and mustache, and sometimes just a mustache. Sometimes he looks older, as I realized, on purpose. Who is he in reality?"

He closed his eyes and rubbed the tightness pulling at his temples. "Even bigger question—who am I, really?"

Her eyes clouded. Her gaze darted to Landon, then back to him. "What do you mean?"

"When he talked about his exciting international trips, friends with yachts, renting villas and someday buying one, I felt… wanderlust, I guess? I knew what kind of projects he talked about. But a few times, I had an adrenaline rush. Like I wanted to try it, too."

"But you haven't." Her voice was soothing.

His fingers tightened around hers. "I was tempted. It was like… like something in my blood made me different from people in this town. My biological father said as much. And that I'm more like him than I realize. You know, among the different jobs I tried over the years, I loved getting training and being a locksmith."

"Why do you say it like there's something… wrong about that?" Her expression intent, she tipped her head to better look at him, every bit of her attentive as if she cared.

"I enjoyed it more than I thought I would. There was something invigorating about hearing that click. I worked for a company people called when they locked themselves out or needed to open a safe and forgot the combination. I caught myself starting to talk to them once I let them inside, noticing the layout or where valuables might be. Chatting them up was so simple. People, especially women, loved the attention." He brought himself into the present and checked on his son.

Meanwhile, she didn't say a word.

He continued, "I had a friend whose father owned a jewelry store, so I started hanging out there, trying to learn the difference between earth-mined precious stones and simulated ones. I had this stirring in my blood, and my dreams filled with scenarios of all the things I could do." He swallowed hard. "My biological father said that was what he used to do. That I would be a natural. He said it with such pride as if I would be continuing in the family's legacy—which is in a way true."

"But you resisted. That's what matters. That says a lot about your character."

Incredible.

She sounded like… like she *admired* him for it!

"Daddy, got another catch!" Landon reeled it in, beaming and without any help.

Pride expanded Kade's chest as the fish plopped into a bucket and he assisted in putting a new worm on the hook.

He returned to his chair. "I had to leave the locksmith's job. I had too much… craving, I guess, inside me. I returned to the only place I could hope to set my head straight. The ranch. Then I fell in love with your sister, and the rest is history."

"I guess there are some things I'm grateful to her for," she muttered.

"My biological father is a skilled manipulator. I've been angry with him for years and still let him back into my life. I want so badly to believe he's a changed man, a remorseful guy who recognized his mistakes and wants to do better. But I'm afraid of what he could do to your mind, to Landon's mind. Parts of the man scare me." He took a deep breath and told her what he didn't want to admit even to himself. "Parts of *me* scare me."

"If we're honest with ourselves, we all do, in one way or another." She brushed the back of her free hand against his cheek, eliciting a different stirring in his blood. "I want to help you. I just don't know how yet. Thank you for telling me this. Maybe we'll figure it out together."

Together.

He liked the word, the sound of it, the taste of it.

Still, cold worry traveled down his spine. "Not the easygoing cowboy you thought you married, huh? Are you disappointed?"

"No. Impressed." Her lips pressed into a pensive line.

Lord, what should I do? Am I being overprotective? Or, like my biological father said, family is family, and you can't get away from it?

"I..." She hesitated.

"Yes?"

"Well, it's by no means a solution, but it would give us a respite." She paused, and he just enjoyed the fact that she used the word *us*. "I know you're busy at work. But could the three of us go for a mini-vacation somewhere, please?"

That beautiful word *us* again. Growing up, he realized fast there was no *us*, only him and whatever family he got thrown in next. After he'd been adopted, he'd only had a few years before becoming an adult and going out on his own.

And while he and Landon had been a team for years now, he couldn't ask his son for advice in such matters.

"I don't like to run away from an issue." Well, based on all his movements and location changes, he liked to run *around* it.

There was a lot of work at the ranch, too, though his family had been pressuring him to have a proper honeymoon.

"It's not running away. It's regrouping and figuring out what to do next. Besides, somebody does owe me a honeymoon, doesn't he?" She winked.

He perked up as he stared over the lake. "I have a month-long vacation saved up, and my family has been insisting on me taking it for a long time. How do you feel about going to a little bungalow on the Texas shore? The dart we threw did hit Texas, don't forget. And Liberty's vacation bungalow has separate bedrooms if you're concerned about that."

Landon jumped, the fishing rod forgotten. "Yay! More fishing! And the ocean! Yay!"

Huh, he'd thought the kid couldn't hear them.

In his excitement, Kade must have spoken louder than he'd

been during the more serious conversation—hopefully.

Still, Kade chuckled. "Well, I like that kind of reaction."

Despite suggesting it, she hesitated and gripped the chair arms.

He was a spontaneous kind of guy, and he liked to travel. But she was the opposite, so maybe she regretted the idea already. Heather admitted she'd never traveled outside Missouri. Besides, he had a new respect for her job.

"I didn't even ask about your work. Do you have a lot of projects?"

When he'd married the first time, he'd thought they would be doing so many things together. Like him, Josephine had been going to the gym and worked out a lot, enjoyed trying new things, and wanted to leave Cowboy Crossing and see the world. She'd made sure to tell him how much they had in common.

But after the wedding, Josephine had traded the gym for plastic surgeries and complained on every trip they'd taken. As for trying new things… "New things" soon grew limited to jewelry and designer clothes.

Marrying a person who'd seemed to share his interests hadn't worked out great. How much more difficult was it going to be with someone so opposite?

"I can take my work with me." Heather looked up at him. "I'm my own boss. I decide how many new projects I want to take on. I've already decided to cut back on my hours to spend more time with you and Landon. Okay, let's go. It all sounds… incredible."

"Yay!" He repeated his son's favorite word and couldn't help it. He drew her into his arms, and Landon joined them.

Dara forgot she was supposed to be quiet, ran to them, and barked.

His chest swelled.

Before the wedding, he'd been dreading spending more time with her. Now he couldn't wait for the vacation to start. He'd needed it for more reasons than one.

She stilled in his embrace and then leaned into him. "Yay it is," she whispered into his shoulder.

His heart expanded.

When she eased out of his embrace—too soon for his liking—she grinned at him.

"My other auntie's house is soooo goooood." Landon drew out the words for emphasis. "Dara loves it, too."

The dog confirmed it with a bark.

Kade nodded. "Liberty already told me we could use it whenever we felt like it." Then he suppressed a grimace. "But she said she'd have to call the fire department there before we go." He gave a demonstrative sigh. "One little fire, not even fire, just some smoke, and people don't trust you."

"One?" She quirked an eyebrow.

"Okay, maybe two. There was an accident when I was a teen. On the bright side, I received some great training in how to use a fire extinguisher afterward."

CHAPTER TWELVE

SATURDAY AFTERNOON, after a short flight and drive in a rental car, Heather stepped inside the bungalow while Kade fetched the bags. Landon "helped" his father by directing which bag should go where from his perch on Kade's shoulders. Dara ran around barking, most likely giving instructions, too.

Getting such a big dog here by plane had no doubt cost Kade a small fortune, but as he'd rightly said, Landon wouldn't be happy without his pet.

This was a place they all could enjoy. The tidy house somehow combined different things that, from one glance, shouldn't go together, and yet they did.

The open-concept interior let them see from the tiled hall into the carpeted living room, where a fireplace beneath a wooden mantle snuggled up next to built-in oak shelves with leather-bound volumes, including books by Mark Twain and posters of jazz musicians and country singers.

She had to smile.

Liberty had transplanted works by famous Missourians to Texas.

"Dad used to read some of these books to us when we were

teens." Kade stopped, Landon's backpack in one hand and his duffel bag in the other. "Now, *those* books stayed in the family library, but Liberty bought a few other editions to reread while on vacation."

Heather's smile widened as she remembered the large library, floor-to-ceiling bookshelves, and comfortable chairs where she'd spent a lot of great hours. "Has she reread them?"

He shook his head. "She loves her job so much she rarely takes vacations. But our friends get good use of this house."

That sounded like Liberty, too.

While Heather's husband—she still couldn't get used to that word—brought in the groceries they'd bought on the way, she wandered to the dining room.

This room looked more like it belonged in a seaside bungalow than the living room had. Oil painted seascapes appeared of good quality, and a tablecloth featuring ships decorated the dining table. A large ship perched on the side table, and a smaller one lay anchored inside a bottle near it.

"Daddy, down. I wanna show Auntie H my room," Landon demanded. Once he was on the floor, he took her hand. "Let's go."

"Meanwhile, I'll unbag our groceries." Kade headed to the kitchen. "Remember, you promised not to do any cooking while on vacation. I'd better not find you near the stove later."

"You're so strict." The corners of her lips curved up, and a warm feeling spiraled through her tummy.

How nice to be pampered in this way!

She followed Landon to his room, not at all surprised to find puppies drawn on the wall or a rug depicting a puppy or the blanket on a small white bed boasting the same pattern. Plush puppy toys greeted her from the desk, bed, and white chair.

Even as a family vacation home, this place exuded friendliness and care, and just like Kade's home, there was that feeling, as though the house wanted to give her a welcome hug.

She helped Landon unpack, tucking his clothes in the nightstand drawers and on the little closet shelves. Though they'd decided to pack light and mostly include necessities, for the child those necessities included more plush puppies.

They were barely done when he darted to the kitchen where Kade finished filling up the fridge.

She smiled at a row of aprons, the smallest one, obviously belonging to Landon, having a puppy appliqué. Despite its coziness, the place still provided modern stainless steel appliances. The towel on the stove handle, as well as salt and pepper shakers in the shape of dogs, offered another nod to the family's favorite boy.

That boy tugged at his father's hand. "Daddy, when are we gonna go to the aquarium?"

Her eyebrows shot up. "What? We're going to buy an aquarium?"

Kade visibly swallowed as he closed the fridge. "Please don't give him any ideas."

"No, silly, we're gonna *go* there. Like inside. They have humongous sharks with humongous teeth!" Landon spread his arms to show how large the sharks were. At least, she sure hoped those were *not* the size of their teeth. "And lots of fish and turtles and birds and… Oh, and stingrays you can pet."

Somehow "stingrays" and "I'd like to pet" didn't go into one sentence. "Sharks? Stingrays?" she squeaked. "I mean, it's safe there, right? We don't have to swim with them, or anything?"

Kade chuckled and wrapped a protective arm around her shoulder. Even after a trip, he smelled good, and his enticing cologne soothed her. "It's perfectly safe."

"Oh, and they also have lots and lots of spiders." The boy's eyes grew big.

Her stomach clenched. "Spiders? They, well, don't escape sometimes, do they?"

Kade shook his head at his son. "Landon, I don't think you

120

need to upsell the aquarium any longer. I'm sure you had her at sharks."

"No kidding," she muttered, her tummy queasy. She dropped into the nearest chair. "Do we... do we have to go?"

"We do! I gotta see those sharks again." The boy stared at her as if she didn't understand something obvious. "I'm gonna treat dogs and fish when I grow up."

"I'm not sure you can do it in that combination," she murmured. And definitely not in Cowboy Crossing.

"Sure I can. I'm gonna be a veteri–vetera—" he stumbled.

"An animal doctor." Kade ruffled his boy's hair.

"Right." Landon nodded. "Like my other auntie and grandma. But grandma retired."

Hmm.

As much as Heather loved spending the time with her husband and son, maybe for this particular project, she could say she needed to work on an assignment or clean the house or... something.

"They also have flamingoes, lionfish, a dolphin show, and I'll be nearby all the time," Kade whispered to her, his breath caressing her skin.

Just like that, her heartbeat went into overdrive.

She smiled. On the other hand, it didn't sound so bad. "I'm in."

Kade returned her smile. "Okay, then. We can go as soon as we shower, change clothes, and get some food in our stomachs."

"Yay!" The boy jumped up and down.

His irresistible enthusiasm widened her smile further.

Or maybe it was something about the way Kade started to look at her these last days and the way he looked at her now. As if he'd come to appreciate her.

Or the way he hugged her often and set her heart aflutter.

Or how much she wanted to be near him, simply be near him. Enough to go near sharks and spiders and maybe even pet a stingray.

She was becoming more adventurous, more open, and more… happy.

"To think about it, I'll take being around spiders to being around my sister any day." Her hand flew to her mouth. "Oh, oops. I didn't mean it."

Kade laughed. "Oh yes, you did. But frankly, I feel the same way. Come on, it's going to be fun."

She looked into his dark eyes where she could lose herself so easily. "Everything is fun when I'm with you." Did she just say that? Yes, she did. "And I mean it, too."

His gaze became serious. "Ditto."

About an hour later, her eyes widened as she strolled through the aquarium's spacious pavilions filled with sea life, her fingers wrapped around Landon's little fingers. Of course, they didn't stay that way for long.

"Sharks!" He darted to his beloved animals.

They had *humongous* teeth indeed, but as they were swimming behind the glass of the floor-to-ceiling tank, she exhaled her relief.

After Landon had seen enough of the sharks, Kade stooped to his child. "How about we go look at flamingoes now?"

"Okay." The boy perked up. "And then pet stingrays, right?"

Kade smiled. "Right." Into her ear, he whispered, "You don't have to pet them."

"Thank you." His hot breath sent a wave of excitement through her.

What was happening to her?

She was behaving like a hormone-charged teenager and not a forty-year-old IT technician in a fake marriage. Okay, she wasn't exactly sure how a forty-year-old IT technician in a fake marriage was supposed to behave. But surely, it wasn't to tremble at nothing more than a glance from her pretend husband.

Soon she stared at rose-colored graceful flamingoes, admiring their beauty. Unlike she'd expected, they weren't in a large cage but in a small pond with plants around it.

"I think this is the most gorgeous bird I've ever seen. Why don't they fly away?" She turned to her—just think about it!—husband.

"Most likely, their wings are clipped. But I prefer to think it's because they like it here and have everything they need." He tucked a strand of hair behind her ear, making her feel like a hormone-struck teenager again, her pulse zapping at an incredible speed.

"Have everything they need... Maybe that's the reason I never left my home state. Except now, of course."

Their gazes met and held, and he seemed to look at her with even bigger admiration than she'd felt looking at flamingoes. "And I traveled to different places because I was always searching for something. I didn't realize before that all I needed, the most precious treasures I could hope for, were always waiting for me in my hometown."

"I'm your treasure, right, Daddy?" The boy's voice made her look at his adorable grinning face.

"Our treasure. Our precious treasure." She crouched and hugged him in earnest, partly because she wanted to, partly because at Kade's words happy tears prickled behind her eyes.

He'd said "treasures."

Plural.

So he meant her, too, right?

As soon as she managed to rein in her emotions, she straightened. "Let's go pet those stingrays."

They entered a large—or as Landon would say, humongous—pavilion where a pool hosted more stingrays than she'd expected. She hesitated.

Despite many children bravely touching stingrays and not

screaming from pain, her stomach quivered. She understood this was completely safe or it wouldn't have been offered. Still, taking another step was difficult.

She glanced at Kade. "I want to show him my support, but…"

"How about we do it the same way as we did with darts? I'll hold your hand in mine, and I'll touch the stingray with the back of my hand? Like this?" He smiled at her, then stroked her face with the back of his hand.

The gesture was fleeting and innocent, but it replaced the quiver of fear in her stomach with fluttering butterfly wings.

She nodded because she couldn't speak. After the wedding, he started to have that effect on her—an effect she didn't know what to do with.

Argh.

She was falling for him, plain and simple.

They walked to the pool, hand in hand.

"Look, they are cute, aren't they?" Landon had no apprehension about petting stingrays. Hopefully, he wouldn't ask to take one home.

"Um, if you say so." She let Kade reach into the water with her hand in his and brush against the closest stingray.

"Are you okay?" His gaze was inquiring.

Was she?

How could she answer?

Mixed emotions assaulted her, far more emotions than she was used to feeling. Feelings of surprise, wonder, gratitude, all rolled into one. She couldn't be mistaken about the interest in his eyes or the caring notes in his voice.

Their connection grew stronger, as though he wanted it to grow. She felt he was changing for the better—or finding better parts of himself because of her—and she was changing because of him, becoming more confident, cheerful, and content.

Thanks to the fake arrangement, they were discovering truths about themselves.

Go figure.

If the thought that one day he'd get tired of her and move on—maybe even go back to her sister!—didn't constantly pass through her mind, her new emotions wouldn't include apprehension.

Lord, if You can hear me… I mean, if You listen… You're not giving me this just to take it away, are You? Or am I living in an illusion like I did with my fiancé?

She waited, but the answer didn't come.

Maybe because she'd seldom prayed, upset with God for giving beauty and popularity to her sister while sparing none for her. Even the fact that she prayed now sent surprise jolting through her.

Kade's faith might be rubbing off on her, if one could say such things about faith.

Well, at least she could treasure this while it lasted. When her heart broke again… Her chest tightened. She'd worry about it then.

She lifted her chin.

"More than okay." She beamed at him. "This is one of the best days of my life. Um, despite the stingrays. I've always resisted stepping out of my comfort zone, trying new things. Apparently, it can be a lot of fun."

Especially if one did them with the people one adored.

Best not to add that.

She was scared to admit, even to herself, how much she was growing to like Kade. She definitely didn't want to admit it to him.

"Let's go, Daddy." Landon had enough of petting stingrays.

"Sure, buddy." Kade hoisted his son on his shoulders, locking him in place.

More warmth loosened her muscles.

Except for Liberty, Heather had stayed away from people in real life, preferring online friendships, especially after boys had teased her or used her to get closer to her popular sister. She'd stopped trusting guys altogether after her fiancé dumped her for her sibling.

Could she trust that Kade wouldn't walk away from her?

"I'm glad." He returned her smile.

A pleasant wave washed over her, and when they left the pavilion and he let her hand go, she wished for the moment to last longer.

Kade glanced at his watch. "We have about half an hour before the dolphin show starts. What else do you want to see?"

"Spiders!" Landon clapped.

Seriously?

Why would they even have arachnids at an aquarium? She shuddered inwardly.

Kade wrinkled his forehead. "How about jellyfish? Aren't they pretty?"

"Okay, Daddy. I'm gonna tell you where to go. I see better from here than you do."

His directions didn't turn out too great, and by the time they found the jellyfish, they had little time left before the dolphin show. So she didn't read the species and descriptions names as she did in other pavilions.

She just looked at the fragile and gorgeous jellyfish—like exquisite beautiful lace. "I heard that some of them are harmful if one gets close." Admiring them from afar was great.

"Why does this remind me of someone?" he muttered.

Maybe she was unfair. "In the jellyfish's defense, they only defend their territory and themselves."

"True. God made them that way." He glanced at his watch again. "Uh-oh, we'd better hurry."

Good thing they'd gotten a map after approaching the wrong pavilion so they knew how to find the open-air show.

They found almost enough space to sit on one of the blue-painted wooden benches—she had to sit very close to Kade, but she didn't mind—and Landon decided not to sit down at all.

For the next minutes, she didn't clap and jump up and down like the boy did, but even her adult and mostly skeptical self was mesmerized by the show.

Dolphins "talked", played with the ball, carried the instructor above the water, and waved farewell with their tail when the show ended.

"They are so smart," she whispered.

Kade leaned to her as they got up to leave. "I read that they have the biggest brain among animals compared to their body mass. And their navigation system exceeds the one given to mankind."

"I didn't know. You're smart, too," she said as they made their way down the stairs.

"Well, that, too, but I read it for Landon's benefit. I might not be book smart, but I'm internet smart."

She was in reality book smart, but she couldn't figure out simple things.

Like how to stop herself from falling for him.

What was she going to do if he decided to leave her in the end?

Her heart squeezed.

She tried to ignore her sister's words replaying in her head— *He never stayed with anyone for long. He'll leave you soon, too.*

Chapter Thirteen

ON THE WAY TO THE BUNGALOW, they stopped at the toy store and bought Landon a plush dolphin. Heather smiled when the boy gave out a delighted yelp. When he said he was going to study the dolphin's anatomy—where did he get such words?—they bought another one, just in case.

When they were back in the rental car, Kade started the engine. "Where would you like to eat? And what would you like to eat for dinner?"

"Seafood!" Landon screamed from the back seat.

"Sounds good to me." She clicked the seat belt closed.

"We're not gonna eat dolphins?" Alarm heightened the boy's squeal.

"No, we're not." Kade chuckled as he drove from the toy store parking lot.

He navigated the city traffic better than she'd expected.

Some time later, they parked near a restaurant at the pier. Signs proclaimed the name of a cartoon character, which Landon pointed out with an approving yell.

Kade opened the door for her, then helped his son out of the harnessed booster seat.

"Are you okay with eating in a fish shack?" He placed his son on his shoulders—by now, she considered it a habit of his.

Or maybe it was a wise decision, considering that, like the little dolphin, Landon was rather curious and could dart somewhere unexpectedly.

"Fish shack?" Delicious tingles ran over her skin from his touch as he took her hand in his. Now she hoped *that* would become a habit of his.

"At the restaurant, they have this outside seating right above the water that people call a fish shack. They also have gorgeous sunsets. And by the way, they harvest their own seafood locally. Everything is fresh and tasty." He led her along a wooden rusty-colored pier to the wooden construction that, true to his words, was above the water.

Though the sun was still up, lanterns along the railings already emitted a soft glow and created magical reflections in the water. Even nearby fishing boats added to the romantic ambiance. People likely came here as much for the atmosphere as for the food, and it wasn't even sunset yet.

The view more than compensated for the simple wooden chairs. As they wove through the tables, her stomach growled at the scents of good ole fried fish, French fries, and the slight tang of lemon. The aroma of hush puppies and freshly baked biscuits set her mouth watering, too.

Once they were seated and given a menu, Kade ordered fried fish and shrimp with French fries and coleslaw, plus iced tea.

One arm pressed over her chubby middle, she sighed. "I'll order a sa—"

Seagulls screamed in protest, and her empty tummy agreed with them. She'd tried to diet several times, and it never seemed to help.

"If you're not sure, we can order a bunch of different dishes, and you're welcome to try from them." Kade gave his menu to the waitress while not taking his eyes from Heather, his smile kind.

"What we don't eat, we'll give to the seagulls," Landon announced.

The seagulls screamed again, this time sounding more in agreement.

The waitress pointed to the sign warning, "Don't feed the seagulls."

"But it would be fun." The boy sighed. "Okay then."

"I'll have mahi-mahi with white rice. A garden salad. And iced tea, unsweetened." She returned the menu to the waitress.

There.

She did order salad, didn't she?

"Are there any dolphins here?" Landon wriggled around and hugged the railing, staring where the water met the sky at the horizon.

"Probably." Kade patted his son on the shoulder, then returned to his place and took her hand, sending that delicious wave through her again.

It *was* becoming a habit of his, and she couldn't be more grateful.

"So you like mahi-mahi?" With the gorgeous view around them, he still looked only at her—while keeping a close eye on his son, of course.

She swallowed. "Honestly, I have no clue what mahi-mahi is. I just decided to be… adventurous. It's fish, right?"

His laughter warmed her. "Yes, it is."

"And… not that kind of raw fish that has to be prepared just right for the people to stay alive after eating it. Right?" It didn't look like a place that served that kind of fish, but one never knew.

"No, it's not. Otherwise, I'd try it for you, and if I stayed alive, then you'd know you could eat it." He winked.

Sometimes she didn't know if he was serious or joking, but hopefully, the wink meant he was joking.

The food soon arrived, and he said grace.

Then he helped his son cut his fish before starting on his own. She tried the mahi-mahi, and her taste buds sang with delight. She did eat the salad, too, which went well with the rest of her food.

"How do you like yours?" Kade wiped some stray tartar sauce from the boy's face.

"Yummy!" The kid saluted him with a French fry.

Kade shared some funny travel stories about the unusual food he'd tried. She listened with fascination, though she was grateful that mahi-mahi turned out to be delicious fish and not a dish of insects like Kade had accidently ordered while traveling in Asia. More than a few times, he made her and Landon laugh.

They chatted so easily. She talked about some fun incidents her clients had with computers and the questions they asked. And he was such a good listener, she'd even mentioned some childhood disappointments. He listened, nodded, smiled, asked questions, and brightened her world the same way the lanterns brightened the evening now.

With their food finished, they lingered, and even Landon stayed still, probably hoping to glimpse a dolphin if he stared at the ocean long enough.

As the sun moved to the horizon in a vivid array of pink, peach, and marmalade, its reflection took her breath away.

Then Kade ran his fingers along the contours of her face.

That could take her breath away anytime, no sunset required.

As she looked at the two amazing guys who'd became her husband and her son—even if "son" was in her soul rather than on paper yet—her heart became fuller with joy than she'd imagined possible.

Could this be what happiness was all about?

Or were these wonderful days simply out-of-the-ordinary miracles?

"Kade!" a shrill voice interrupted her thoughts. "Is that you?"

A young well-shaped woman—that shape showcased extremely well by a skimpy white tank and blue jean cut-off shorts—charged toward them. Heather swallowed hard.

Maybe the woman wasn't drop-dead gorgeous like Heather's sister, but no doubt she was attractive. And very, very slim.

Kade grimaced as if he'd just eaten something sour, but then he plastered on a smile and got up. "Hello, Maude. Let me introduce my wife, Heather. And this is my son, Landon."

The woman seemed to deflate like a balloon. "Oh. You got married again? Well, sorry I missed my chance." She whirled around and stomped away. On the way, she muttered something like, "Can't believe he'd marry someone like that."

"Who was that, Daddy?" Landon asked what Heather wished she was brave enough to.

"Um, I used to date her once. Are you ready to go, or would you like a dessert?" He clearly tried to change the topic.

"I'm full, Daddy. Let's go." Landon must've given up on the possibility of seeing dolphins tonight.

It would take two of that woman to make one Heather.

She cringed. "Definitely no dessert for me."

As Kade gestured to the waitress for the bill, Heather blurted out, "Interesting. We're many miles away from home, our first day in a different state, and you bump into someone you dated. If we went to Alaska, would we meet someone you dated there, too?"

"I've never been to Alaska."

"But if you had, you'd have dated every single woman miles around. Considering the population isn't dense there, you'd cover a lot of miles." Her hand pressed to her mouth to stop anything more emerging.

She didn't need to infuse her voice with so much sarcasm. She knew his reputation, and it wasn't like he'd encouraged that woman.

On the contrary, he'd immediately introduced Heather as his

wife.

Argh.

She was making a scene, and worse, she was doing it in front of his son.

Her face flamed, hot enough the chef here could grill fish on it.

Maybe what hurt her the most wasn't meeting one of his previous flames, but hearing the woman's words—*I can't believe he'd marry someone like that.*

A muscle moved in his jaw. "Listen to me. If I wanted to be with this woman or some other woman, why would I marry you?"

Like that was a comforting question!

She rolled her eyes at the answer. "Because I asked."

Besides, he did it for his son and not for her, but she couldn't add that in Landon's presence.

The waitress brought the bill, and Kade gave his credit card.

As soon as the waitress left, he bent across the table. "Right now, right here, I'm with you. It's all that should matter."

It wasn't, and a lump formed in her throat.

It was such a wonderful evening, but the pleasant feeling she'd had melted like ice in her glass. She didn't have the reassurance of his love. She was a fake wife who'd blackmailed him to marry her, taking advantage of his paternal love.

She'd probably pay for it with a broken heart.

"Auntie H, are you okay?" Landon tugged at her hand. "You're not leaving us. Are you? Please don't go."

His lower lip trembled. His mother leaving him behind like something unwanted had left its mark, and that had to be the reason he was clinging to her now.

Suppressing a stab of guilt, she scooted to him and smiled when she wanted to cry. "I'm not leaving. I'm okay. I'm sorry, Landon. It's fine. Really."

Landon nodded, though not looking convinced, and she

scolded herself.

They made it to the rental car in silence.

His jaw set tight, Kade helped his son into the harnessed booster seat in the back. She didn't wait for him to open the door for her but slipped inside.

He took the driver's seat and reached for her hand. "Heather, I wouldn't cheat on you. Don't you know that?"

"I know." She clicked her seat belt closed and looked away.

The issue wasn't that physically he was way more attractive than she was or that he'd been a womanizer. The real issue was that she was terrified to fall for someone who'd never give his heart to her.

It wasn't his fault, but hers.

Though some men defined "cheat" differently. He wouldn't communicate with some of his old flames, would he? Surely not.

Jealousy made her wince. Just because her ex-fiancé had dated her sister behind her back for a while—they'd claimed they'd done it in secret because they didn't want to hurt her feelings—didn't mean other men would do the same.

Her phone vibrated in her pocket.

If not for the embarrassing scene at the restaurant, she'd let it go to voice mail. If it was Liberty, her best friend wouldn't mind her calling back. And she didn't want to do business during her vacation. This was a time set aside to give her attention to her husband and son.

However, the call was perfectly timed if she needed something to shift her thoughts from the line they were taking. Her lips curved up a little at the name on the screen. Stewart Del Bosque.

One of her favorite clients.

A good distraction when her trust in her husband seemed to be falling apart before she'd even had time to build it.

Well, maybe she was too distracted because when she swiped the screen to answer, she pressed the speakerphone button. "Hello,

Stewart." She glanced back and kept her voice down as the boy drifted to sleep. She reduced the volume, too. No need to fumble with turning the speakerphone off. Her client knew better than to talk important business on the phone, and she didn't have secrets from her husband.

"Hello, Heather! Man, I missed hearing from you." The rich baritone filled the car's cabin. But then, everything about that guy was rich.

"Glad to hear it."

"I have an important project, and I need a team of geniuses to work on it. You're on the top of my list. Actually, you're the only name on my list—there aren't that many geniuses around." He chuckled. "Except for myself, of course."

The man never lacked confidence. But then, you couldn't blame someone for being confident when he'd built a fortune in less than a decade.

She stared out the window at the lanterns they passed. "I'm flattered—really—but you'll have to find someone else."

"I wouldn't have made it as far as I did if I didn't hire the best. I might not understand much about computer programs and computers in general. But from the work you've done for me and from what I was told, you're it. You know the compensation would be significant."

His praise soothed her damaged self-esteem, and she sat up straighter. "It's not that."

"You can work from home. Or I can send a private jet and fly you here. You'll have your own penthouse. It doesn't have to be all work. I'll take you to the best restaurants. Caviar, strawberries, and chocolate will be delivered to your room daily. Lots of chocolate." The voice turned smooth like the dessert he'd mentioned.

Was that a gasp on Kade's part?

Satisfaction zinged through her. "I can't. Really. I just got married."

"Wow. Well, congratulations." A sigh reverberated down the line. "I should've made my move a long time ago, shouldn't I? I hope the man knows what a treasure he has. Whenever you're back from your honeymoon, let me know. I'm not a person who gives up easily, at least, when it comes to work."

"Thank you and thank you." She swiped the screen to disconnect the call, feeling a little lighter.

This was what she needed, even if he didn't mean the part about "making his move."

"For the record, 'The man knows what a treasure he has.' If it's okay to ask, who was that?" Was a jealous note curdling Kade's voice, or was it her wishful thinking?

She shrugged nonchalantly. "Someone I did a few projects for. Stewart Del Bosque."

"Are you serious? *The* Stewart Del Bosque? I guess there aren't too many, so it must be."

She pressed a finger to her lips and gestured back with her other hand. "Shhh. Landon is sleeping." Then she nodded.

"Right. Wow." Kade kept his voice low now. "Private jet, huh? Caviar and chocolate? Is there something I need to know about the two of you?"

Okay, now there was no doubt about the jealousy.

And fine, unworthy though it was, another jolt of satisfaction zipped through her.

It wasn't so simple when the roles were switched, was it?

CHAPTER FOURTEEN

"HMM..." HEATHER SHIFTED IN HER SEAT, just enough to face him. "I could ask you the same question, but it would take years for you to tell me about all the women you dated. As for me, I can sum this up quickly. I did freelance work for this guy for years and only communicated with him online and via FaceTime. Never flirted with him. In fact, I don't know how to flirt."

"I know you don't." His voice softened.

Huh.

Should she be insulted or flattered? "Still, you react in this way. Now consider how I see it. Even here, we met one of your exes. In Cowboy Crossing, wherever we go, we'll run into someone you've dated. From what I heard, a lot of them think your marriage won't last and they'll have a chance with you. I know you don't give them a reason to believe that, but how do you think it makes me feel?"

"I... hadn't thought about it."

She stretched toward him across the console as much as her seat belt allowed. "Listen to me. Right here, right now, I'm with you. That's all that should matter."

"Huh. Okay. Sans private jet, I can give you caviar and

chocolate. Every day. All the time, if you'd like." His voice became more cheerful as he slowed around a curve.

A burst of laughter slipped loose before she quieted it and checked the back seat. Landon was still sleeping. Kade didn't know she was so close to giving him her heart without caviar and chocolate. "Sans the scene at the restaurant, you're already making me happy. Every day. All the time."

Hmm, the drive was taking rather longer than she wanted, maybe because they had to go slow through the traffic and the bungalow was on the beach, outside city limits. She missed Cowboy Crossing with its shorter distances and limited traffic.

"I'm glad and grateful to God for it. Because I didn't expect it, but you already make me happy, too. All the time." He stopped at a red light.

Then he brushed the back of his hand against her cheek. "Every day I discover something new about you, and it's always fascinating. It makes me cherish you more and more. And the way you treat my son fills me with gratitude."

"I love that kid."

He moved forward on the green light. "I get a feeling you worry about your extra pounds, but I couldn't care less about them. It's all about the way your smile lights up your face and illuminates something inside me. It's about how brilliant and humble you are at the same time. You even turned down a high-paying job to stay with us. It's about your kindness and loyalty. Frankly, I could talk about everything I admire about you for hours and still find something to say."

That was all it took for her insides to turn mushy. She had a ridiculous wish for him to stop the car, park somewhere, and kiss her senseless.

Her blood ran faster in her veins just at the thought.

But she couldn't read too much into his words. He hadn't declared his love, he'd just talked of admiring her character.

Holding tight to that reminder, she listened to him tell her more about his childhood. Soon they pulled into the driveway.

For a few moments, they lingered, and her gut tightened over some of his heart-wrenching experiences. That he'd come through that to become the man he was today, setting a great example for his son, was nothing short of remarkable.

While Kade carried his half-asleep son into his room and helped him change into his pajamas, she brushed her teeth. It seemed important to have fresh breath—and she preferred to think it was purely for hygienic purposes.

She brushed her hair because, well, it was a little tangled.

Sprinkling some perfume on her wrists didn't have a logical reason, and therefore didn't deserve pondering over.

She rushed to the child's room so she could tuck him in, too.

Huh.

Now Landon's eyes were wide open.

"Auntie H, tell me a story." He grinned at her.

Hmm, she was good with computers, but a storyteller she was not. Back in Missouri, they had plenty of children's books, but they didn't bring any here. Oops.

Kade got up and gestured for her to take the honorary place at the side of the kid's bed.

Racking her brain, she sat down. "What would you like the story to be about?"

"A little dolphin." The grin widened.

Something about that smile, open and sincere, just like his father's, melted her heart. Well, hopefully, she'd earn that grin, but even more, she hoped he'd fall asleep before she had to tell an entire story.

Kade shifted to her, giving her a whiff of his enticing cologne. "I can look up something on the internet."

He guessed her dilemma. He could read her as if they'd been married for years.

Goodness!

Heat prickled the back of her neck. She sure hoped he couldn't read some of the thoughts she shouldn't be having.

Like how much she wanted him to lean even closer, claim her lips with his, and…

She cleared her throat. "Once upon a time, a little dolphin lived in the ocean with his parents and other little dolphins and their parents, and, well, other relatives." Maybe she could name all the relatives until his eyes would get droopy? "Two aunts, two uncles, five cousins…"

Maybe not. She swallowed.

Kade placed a hand on her shoulder, making her feel the warmth of his touch even through the cotton fabric of her T-shirt. "It was a curious little dolphin. He wanted to see the far ends of the ocean. He wanted to see sunshine and jump out of the water."

Landon nodded, snuggling back lower into his bed with a drowsy whisper about today being the *best* day ever.

Together, they ended up telling the story of how the little dolphin lost track of his parents and other dolphins but, in the end, they found each other because they had a great "system of navigation."

Thankfully, they didn't have to explain what a system of navigation was to the child because, by then, his eyes were closed and his breathing evened out, a content smile soothing his face as he snuggled next to his new toy.

They tiptoed out of the room and Kade closed the door.

Her breathing caught as she stared into his eyes in the dim hall light. She didn't want to say goodnight and let the evening end. But she'd heard more than enough rumors about him, seen enough with her own eyes.

With just one exception, as soon as Kade conquered someone's heart, he lost interest in that woman.

She couldn't let him know she was about to hand him her

heart on a silver platter.

He lingered, as well.

Did he feel the same irrational longing?

"How about I make us iced tea, and we take it to the patio and watch the moonlight and stars?" He ran his fingers through her hair—she was glad she'd brushed it!

A pleasant feeling spread through her body, then pooled in the pit of her stomach. "I'd love that."

Minutes later, they were outside, sitting in metal patio chairs cushioned with dolphin-patterned pillows, sipping on iced tea.

She took a deep breath of fresh salty air as the breeze danced on her skin. Moonlight shimmered on restless waves, the ocean's whisper a soothing backdrop to the restlessness in her blood.

But even more beautiful were Kade's eyes in the light-blue lantern light, and the longing she sensed rather than saw in them. Surely that wasn't her wishful thinking.

"You look amazing tonight." He returned his empty glass to the table and shifted toward her.

She nearly snorted.

Amazing, right.

Probably the dim light helped. But the admiration in his eyes confirmed his words.

Huh.

Why was she defensive?

Okay, she knew why, but that needed to change. She needed to grow confident about more than her professional skills—she had plenty of confidence there—but also about her attractiveness. Or something even deeper than that—her self-worth. Something based on more than how she looked or on doing a good job.

The opinion of that woman in the restaurant shouldn't matter. Or her sister's cruel teasing. Or what her bullying classmates had called her.

What mattered was what Kade thought of her.

What she thought of herself.

She set her glass beside his, got up, and stared at the ocean.

Partly to drink in the serenity, let it fill her lungs, seep into her pores, slow her blood, exactly what she needed for her raw nerves.

Partly to distract herself because staring in Kade's eyes created an unwanted craving.

Like how much she wanted all this to be real.

For their marriage to be real.

He wrapped his arms around her middle, having come up silently behind her, and a wave of excitement swept her up.

His proximity sharpened her senses. The murmur of the ocean—and her heartbeat—grew louder, his cologne and the salty air more enticing.

But staying in his arms would be a mistake.

She eased out of his embrace and turned to him. This was even a bigger mistake. As she stared in his dark eyes, she saw a silent question. She saw admiration, longing, and things she didn't want to recognize, or rather, didn't dare to believe.

Their gazes met and held, and her heartbeat skyrocketed.

She should've gone to her room. She shouldn't be here, alone with Kade, without Landon providing a buffer, a reminder not to get too close.

Excitement quickened her breath as her husband—husband!—drew her closer.

Despite her wise intentions, she leaned into him.

Right here.

Right now.

With the breeze caressing her skin and the ocean murmuring in the background. In Kade's arms. There was no other place where she'd rather be.

His voice became husky. "I can't explain this, but you mean more and more to me every day. No, wrong."

"Wrong?" She stilled.

"You mean more and more to me every minute."

"Ditto." Unlike him, she'd never been eloquent.

"If you want me to step away, you need to tell me now." His voice dipped lower, and so did his gaze, to her lips, before he looked into her eyes again.

She was going to remind him that their marriage was a pretend one. That they needed a list of rules, and not kissing should be number one on the list. That nothing was going to happen between them. That…

"I don't want you to step away." Did she just say that?

Apparently, that was all the encouragement he needed. He dipped his head and claimed her lips, and it was nothing like she'd imagined it.

It was far, far better.

An invisible ocean wave seemed to sweep her up and carry her away into a world where she was admired and cherished.

Every cell in her body sang with delight. She'd rarely been kissed, and she'd never been kissed like Kade kissed her. As she raised herself on tiptoes and wrapped her arms around his neck, she felt as light as the foam on the top of a wave, as though she could disappear into the thin air.

Something changed inside her as she responded to him with everything there was in her. With every delightful moment, she wanted to believe a future together was possible.

When he finally let her go, she couldn't think and struggled to breathe.

Just one thought pulsed through her, like an erratic heartbeat.

This was the man for her.

It would be naïve to believe this, but everything—especially his kisses—felt so right when she was in his arms.

This.

Was.

The.

Man.

For.

Her.

"That was incredible. You… are incredible." His eyes darkened.

She needed to get a grasp on reality. "You've probably said that to every woman you've kissed."

And there were a lot of them. That was the reality.

She looked away.

The issue wasn't that he had a past but that she lacked the confidence to be with a man like him.

"No, I've never said that to any other woman. I pray one day you'll see yourself the way I see you now. You need to learn to love yourself the way you are. Until you do, you and I don't stand a chance." His voice changed, became more distant. "As much as I'd like to stay out here, I have to go back indoors. I don't want Landon to wake up and become scared."

She nodded.

Was this because he was a caring dad? Or because she kept bringing up things she shouldn't, kept ruining everything?

Even the magic of their kiss.

A part of her was reluctant to return, but he was right. They should go in.

She wouldn't want the boy to wake up and find the place empty, not realizing they were on the patio. Kade was a good father, and his care for his son was one of many things that attracted her to him.

"Go ahead. I'll follow you soon." Her mind still reeling from the kiss, she turned to let the ocean breeze cool her heated skin, to let the view cool her heated mind.

What was happening to her?

Deep inside, she knew the answer.

She just didn't want to acknowledge it.

The ocean seemed endless, and the shore stretched in front of her. Neither offered an escape from the equally endless emotions growing inside her.

CHAPTER FIFTEEN

KADE WENT TO BED, thinking of kissing Heather and how much he wanted to do it again. Then he'd dreamed of her, and she was his first thought when he woke up.

He shouldn't have kissed her. Things were much simpler before. He'd never given kissing a woman much importance, apart from a shallow pride in his skills.

With Heather, however, it was all different. She was already his wife, and yet not till last night had they shared their first kiss. A pleasant sensation surged through his veins at the memory.

He'd find such a wait ridiculous if someone told him, but he'd learned to be patient with her. With her, a kiss was a promise indeed.

A promise of commitment and love, and he couldn't give her that.

Not yet.

But a man had only so much willpower. He had none at all when he was lost in those baby blues of hers, seeing them filled with hope and longing.

It was different with her. Almost... sacred.

He felt a changed man with her, and she was like no other

woman he'd ever met. Her fragile self-esteem and humility both attracted and scared him.

Men like us don't stay with one woman for long.

He checked his phone and smiled. No missed calls from his biological father. Since he'd told him about the vacation, the man had left him alone.

A respite he needed, but what would happen next? A burning sensation formed inside his chest, and he rubbed at his breastbone. How could he figure out what his father wanted—what he was capable of—when he couldn't even figure out his own feelings?

He got out of bed, shaved, and brushed his teeth fast, enjoying the toothpaste's fresh mint flavor. Then he gave Dara fresh water and biscuits.

Hmm. He liked the idea of making breakfast. But not so much the thought of his family waking up to the fire brigade's siren.

He patted Dara, then walked to the child's room and checked on his son. Sound asleep.

That sight never failed to warm his heart. He closed the door, and another idea came to him. But to pull it off he needed to—

He stumbled into Dara in the hall as he returned to his room. They'd trained her to keep quiet and avoid barking, so she didn't wake up the boy. Maybe they'd trained her too well.

As soon as he regained his equilibrium, Heather emerged from her room and bumped into him.

Her hair was tousled adorably, and her puppy-pattern pajamas were beyond cute. He even liked the sleepy look in her eyes. It reminded him of the ocean. Of the desire filling his every cell as he'd brushed his lips against hers.

When she didn't wear her glasses, like now, he could see tiny azure specks in her eyes, and he could lose himself in those baby blues as easily as he'd lost himself in the incredible sensations of yesterday's kiss. The aftereffects still made his blood rush faster.

"Good morning, my darling wife." A wave of pleasure spread

through him at the feel of her in his arms.

They were total opposites, and still, they fit so well together. As if God had designed them for each other.

Whoa.

Where did that thought come from?

She looked up at him. "My darling wife, huh?"

"Well, that's what you are." His reluctant decision to marry her could turn out to be the best decision of his life.

"Let your darling wife pass so she can make you and Landon breakfast." She either didn't remember the amazing moments they'd shared yesterday or didn't want to.

Either possibility tightened his gut.

Dara, tired of waiting patiently for her people to notice her, thrust herself between them and licked Heather's hand.

That at least brought a smile to Heather's face. "And feed Dara, of course. What would you like for breakfast?"

Heather cooking for them wasn't part of his idea. "Hold on. I already fed Dara. Are you hungry?"

She shook her head.

"Is there something you could do this morning? And could you watch Landon, please?"

"Yes and yes. I have a project pending, and I could work on my laptop." She folded her arms across her chest as her eyes narrowed. "Is there someplace else you need to be?"

He could explain it all to her, but then it wouldn't be a surprise, would it? "I'll be back soon."

He wanted to kiss her on the cheek, or even better, repeat yesterday's kiss. But based on her frown, it might not end well.

He changed from his baggy pajama bottoms into jeans and T-shirt fast and was out the door in no time. Once in the rental car, he did an internet search and set up the GPS.

Finding everything he wanted in the neighboring city wasn't easy, but now, he was back in the bungalow, several bags in hand.

He opened the door and crept into the kitchen.

Apparently, not stealthily enough.

"Daddy!" Landon darted to him, still in his sweet pajamas.

"Good morning, buddy." He lifted his son and threw him in the air, eliciting several delightful yelps, before placing the boy on the beige tile floor.

Dara ran into the kitchen, barking as if she'd figured that once the boy was up and screaming she didn't have to be quiet any longer.

Unlike the boy and the dog, Heather, with her eyes narrowed again, didn't look enthusiastic. "I gave him a glass of orange juice, a banana, and an apple. And we took Dara outside." Her gaze slid to the bags. "Oh… You went shopping?"

"Yes, for you. What did you think I was going to do?" He blinked, then recalled the scene at the restaurant. "You didn't think—"

She tipped her chin. "Of course, I didn't."

Riiight.

"Well, let me organize things here," he indicated the bags in his hands, "so we can eat breakfast."

"I'll get us drinks. What would you like?"

He breathed in the aroma of freshly made coffee as he emptied the bags. "Coffee would be great. Black."

"I know." She poured him a mug. Then she poured two glasses of orange juice, too.

Something shifted inside him, an empty space now filled.

A family breakfast with everybody smiling. Pure bliss. He could get used to this.

She knew how he liked his coffee, what he wanted for dinner, and how much he loved his son. But she had no clue he was falling for her.

Who'd think that a woman with tousled hair and zero makeup could look so appealing, especially when wearing whimsical pajamas? She smelled of coffee, apples, and new possibilities. He had a nearly irresistible urge to take her into his arms and kiss her senseless again.

Instead, he concentrated on making sandwiches.

Her eyes widened when she saw the things on the table. Then she started laughing, the sound music to his ears. "You didn't!"

"I sure did. I keep my promises. Caviar, strawberries, and chocolate. Lots of chocolate." He took the toy airplane and handed it to his son. "This wouldn't qualify as a private jet, of course. But it was as close as I could get on such short notice."

Making engine noises, Landon moved the little toy plane in the air as if it were flying. "I'm gonna be a pilot when I grow up." Then he seemed to remember something and grinned. "No, I'm gonna teach dolphins to do tricks and learn how to make them better when they're sick, like Auntie Liberty does with the cows and horses."

Kade returned the grin as he pulled the chair out for her, then helped Landon scramble into his chair. His boy never failed to make him smile. "Dolphins, huh?"

Heather touched her pajamas as she sat down. "Something tells me we're going to be shopping for matching dolphin-patterned pajamas soon."

He chuckled as he joined her at the table. "I might get one, too. At least, the pajama pants."

"Yeah! I wanna work with dolphins." Landon munched a caviar sandwich. Surprisingly, the kid who was so fussy about his food normally chowed down the salty caviar.

His heart expanding, Kade hugged his little boy. He'd miss him dearly when his son left their hometown eventually, but he wouldn't hold him down, either. "Whatever you want, buddy. Follow your dreams."

"I wonder what would happen to me, how far I'd go if I had encouraging parents like that." Heather lifted a chocolate candy from the box, then put it back.

"Well, what would you want to do? Where would you want to go?" He studied her.

If she discovered she wanted to go somewhere far away, would he follow her?

Strangely enough, now he couldn't imagine being separated from her, even for a day.

Who'd think?

Him, the guy who'd never liked to settle down in the same place or with the same person. Especially with the same person. After all, sooner or later, people left, and it was easier to leave first.

Bits of caviar from his sandwich popped beneath his tongue, though his thoughts kept him so busy he forgot to savor the taste. He made another sandwich and added it to Landon's plate.

"I don't know." Heather picked up another chocolate. This time, she bit into it. "Mmm, this is good. Thank you." She paused, either to think or to savor the chocolate, most likely both. "Actually, I do know. I'd still stay in my hometown and become a freelance IT and software developer doing website design from time to time. Exactly what I'm doing now."

He recalled her conversation yesterday with the billionaire and sipped his coffee to chase away the bitterness. "You excel at it." He didn't mean to sound so dry.

He refilled Landon's cup with OJ and added strawberries to his plate, their tangy scent mingled with the aroma of coffee. He grinned. Landon loved strawberries.

There was no reason for jealousy to tinge their delicious breakfast with bitterness.

On the contrary, having other guys admire her, especially such successful guys, should make him value her more.

Say it with more conviction this time. "You really have done well. I'm proud of you." He gulped his coffee, then helped himself to another caviar sandwich.

"Thank you. That means a lot to me. When I was growing up, it hurt me at first that I never could go anywhere because all our finances were spent on my sister. Then I got used to it and accepted it. I never had an outgoing personality or a wandering spirit, anyway. But sometimes I wondered at everything I missed, and it bothered me. You made me see I didn't miss anything important. I mean, I like this vacation, but I look forward to returning to Cowboy Crossing, too. I'm right where I want to be."

His heart warmed until he realized she didn't add, "I'm right with who I want to be with."

"I'm full." Landon pushed the empty plate away and settled on the rug with his new jet.

While she left the kitchen and returned with more of Landon's toys, Kade drained his coffee, enjoying its richness. "At first, I resented my life back in my hometown, but I loved my boy enough to settle in. Then, like you, I got used to it and accepted it. It took me a while to realize that I grew to love my work, our community, my family's support, and of course my child."

He'd never expected it, but marrying Heather was healing the heart her sister had broken. Or maybe it had already started healing, and he hadn't noticed until now. He made himself another caviar sandwich.

She sipped her orange juice and studied him over the rim. "I'm glad. Are *you* where you want to be?"

Scooting forward, he set the sandwich on his plate, edged it aside, and folded his arms on the countertop. "I am."

Maybe he was even *with the person* he wanted to be with, besides his precious child, but the feeling was so new and fragile he didn't say it out loud.

"Me, too!" Landon voted with his toy jet. "Oh, I wanna see that ship Auntie H told me about." His eyes grew big. "That's where *I* wanna be today. People can visit it, right? And it has

152

planes on the deck. Lots and lots of planes. Hmm. Maybe I gonna be a pilot, too. I wanna learn to fly."

Kade stooped to his boy. "You don't want to be a veterinarian any longer? What are dolphins and puppies going to do without you?"

She couldn't help giggling as if watching these two gave her more joy than eating caviar and chocolate—that was saying something.

"Huh." The boy hugged his plush dolphin. "I'm gonna be a flying vete–vere—animal doctor."

She gave Kade an apologetic smile. "He wanted me to go on the internet to look up interesting things we could do in the city. Visiting the ship appeared a good idea. I hope it doesn't change any of your plans."

He plucked a chocolate from the dish and plopped it on his tongue, staying silent while it melted. "Sounds great to me. I was thinking about taking him there, too. We just need to wear comfortable shoes because there's going to be a lot of walking."

She ate a strawberry. "About learning to fly. For a long time, I felt like I was stuck. That I couldn't fly, like I was never given wings. Thanks to getting to know you, I don't feel that way anymore."

"God gives all people wings. But some people choose to clip them." Was that what he'd done for a while? Was he clipping his own wings by not letting himself fall for any woman, especially after his ex had broken his heart?

Yesterday, when he'd kissed Heather, he'd felt like he could lift himself in the air, like he'd been flying a plane or something. But in the end, he'd stopped himself.

Yes, he'd pulled away because of his son. But a tiny part of him wanted to stop himself before his attraction to his wife grew any deeper.

Yes, she was his *wife*. But he knew firsthand, from his

experience and his brother's experience, that marriage didn't last. Even passionate love didn't last.

Could this, the combination of attraction, friendship, and companionship last longer, for all their sakes?

She seemed to read his thoughts as she drained her orange juice. "Maybe I'm clipping my wings in this relationship. Or maybe it's you who is clipping your own wings. Oh, look, we might have something in common."

He chuckled without mirth. "Looks like it. Really, we have more things in common. Like loving Landon."

She nibbled on another strawberry. "Plus dedication to work, kindness to others—"

Dara barked.

Heather laughed. "Love for dogs…"

Landon leaped to his feet. "I'm ready. Let's go see the ship! Pretty please?"

About an hour later, they were walking aboard the large World War II aircraft carrier located right in the bay. The ocean sparkled in the bright summer sun, glazing the water with a golden tint.

First, they walked to the hangar deck and explored passages.

"I'm grateful I wore jeans instead of a dress," she muttered, and made sure to go last when they climbed upstairs. "I wish I ate less the last two weeks—make it the last two years."

"Oh, come on." He shook his head. When would this beautiful woman realize her dress size didn't matter?

"It isn't that the passages are that narrow, but I have an irrational worry I might get stuck," she whispered at the bottom of the stairs. "You know, like Winnie-the-Pooh after visiting the Rabbit."

He laughed. Usually, her self-criticism irritated him, but he had to admit there was something appealing about her self-deprecating humor. "I'd pull you out. Give me your hand."

He pulled her up, true to his word, not that she came anywhere near getting stuck. They explored the bridge, the captain's quarters, and then one of the cabins.

"Are you tired?" He looked at his son, then at her.

"No!" they chimed in unison.

"Let's go see planes!" Landon snatched his hand and dragged him toward the aircraft.

"I read in the brochure they have twenty airplanes." Rather than the planes filling the deck, her head turned toward the shimmering sea and the cloudless sky. "Wow, what a gorgeous view."

He marveled at her smile, far more gorgeous than any view. "It really is."

She swatted his hand. "Oh, come on," she repeated his words.

"I mean it." And he did.

Even with a magnificent bay around them, basking in the afternoon sunshine, all he wanted to look at was Heather.

After several hours of exploring the planes, reading about them, and taking pictures, he turned to Landon and Heather. "They have a mess hall here. Or we can eat at a restaurant somewhere else. What would you like?"

"Let's eat here!" Landon clapped.

Heather nodded.

After chili dogs with fries and glasses of iced tea, they headed back to the rental car.

"Best day ever!" Landon announced, skipping alongside them.

Kade smiled. He lived for these kinds of words from his son. "Didn't you say that yesterday?"

"Oh." The boy thought a moment. "Today is bester!"

When Kade laughed, Heather joined him. "Better," he corrected once he stopped laughing.

Landon nodded. "That, too."

His phone beeped in his pocket as they neared his rental car, and he pulled it out of his pocket. His heart dipped when he opened the screen and read the message from his biological father.

SON, SOME THINGS CHANGED. WE NEED TO TALK SOON.

He suppressed a frown. *We need to talk* never meant anything good.

"My father says he wants to talk soon, but hopefully, it can wait." Another incoming message made him cringe.

This one was from his ex.

RUN ALL YOU WANT, BUT I'M GOING TO FIND YOU. AND I'M GOING TO GET WHAT I WANT.

His bliss vanished.

He stopped, then resumed his pace when Landon tugged at his hand. He didn't want to mention Josephine in front of his son.

Well, hopefully by the time Josephine interrupted their lives, Heather would be confident in their relationship and marriage, and it wouldn't threaten her sense of security.

As for his biological father...

Premonition squeezed Kade's heart again, and he didn't have an explanation for it.

"He wouldn't hurt his grandson, right?" Heather's forehead creased.

His concern must have shown on his face. Either that, or she could read his mind. She touched his hand, and the tightness around his chest loosened.

"I hope not. But he hurt me, though he told me some pretty good excuses trying to justify it." He pressed on the key fob to open the rental car.

After everyone piled in, Heather buckled his son in the booster seat, and Kade drove away from the bay, she reached for his hand again, sending a fragile tenderness all the way to his heart. "Landon is right, you know. Yesterday was the best day ever, and today is even *bester*."

His sense of dread evaporated, thanks to both her touch and her words. They were building something precious here.

Something he couldn't even dream of, didn't ask for, didn't hope to have after his difficult childhood and teens and disastrous marriage. But God gave it to him.

Lord, please help us not ruin what we have, what we're building. And… thank You.

Between his abandonment issues and her trust issues—and upcoming "pleasant" visits from his ex and father—they'd need all the help they could get.

Keeping his attention on the road, he brought her fingers to his lips and kissed every one of them. "I look forward to even *bester* days to come."

Chapter Sixteen

THE NEXT DAY, Kade woke up to the enticing aromas of coffee and bacon drifting from the kitchen. He jumped out of bed, changed into jeans and a T-shirt, and rushed to the kitchen.

He usually awakened early. Days at the ranch started early, especially in summer.

Why had he overslept?

"Daddy!" Landon leaped from the kitchen chair and hugged his legs while Dara greeted him with a bark but stayed at her place in the hall.

"Good morning, buddy." He lifted his son and nuzzled his nose, making him laugh, then put him back on the chair.

"Good morning, Daddy." Landon added another piece to his puzzle featuring German shepherd puppies.

"Daddy, can we get a new puzzle with dolphins? Please?" The boy looked up and grinned.

His heart swelling, Kade ruffled his son's soft hair. He needed to develop resistance to that grin. And he would. Just not right now. "Sure. I mean, I hope the local store has them. If not, we'll order online."

"Good morning." Heather glanced up from the skillet as

sunlight filtered through white curtains.

"Good morning, my darling wife." He placed a kiss on her cheek, enjoying how a blush touched her face and her eyes lit up. "And what a good morning it is, indeed."

Just like his son's grin, her smile reached deep into his heart, only in a different way. There was something incredible about starting his morning with a contented grin from his son, cheerful barking from his dog, and a luminous smile from his wife.

A hearty breakfast with bacon, eggs, and hash browns wouldn't hurt, either.

"I told you not to cook anything while on vacation, though." He wagged his finger at her.

Laughter danced in her eyes as she played a pout. "You're such a strict husband. But you've been so nice I wanted to do something nice for you and Landon."

Dara barked.

"And Dara. Oh, and I already fed and walked her."

Belatedly, he remembered he didn't even ask. Then something akin to hope eased the weight from his shoulders, the tension from his muscles. He was used to doing this all on his own and okay with it, really. But having someone to share that load with—willingly—and even enjoy it, having someone walk on the path beside him made him feel lighter and, as Landon would say, bester.

"Let's set the table, son." He picked up the box to tuck the puzzle away.

"Okay." His son nodded and scooped the puzzle into its box.

As they proceeded to set the table, thoughts whirled through Kade's mind.

When they'd lived in California with his ex, Landon had been difficult, even thrown tantrums, and that behavior had continued after they returned to Missouri, sans Josephine.

After Heather had reappeared in their lives, the boy changed. Tantrums became rare, and his mood and willingness to do things right had improved.

Kade had attributed that to the child's resilience and getting used to the new life, as well as to being close to the boy's grandmother, aunt, and uncle, thrilled about the positive change.

How come he hadn't realized he had a happy, well-adjusted son in many ways thanks to Heather?

Gratitude overwhelming him, he walked to her, waited until she turned off the stove, and hugged her, breathing the flowery perfume coming from her hair. "Thank you."

"For what?" Eyes widening, she tipped her face his way.

"For everything. For my son. For us. For you being you. For the new me." He wanted to linger with her in his arms, just stay there holding her close as if that could prove she wouldn't disappear like other people dear to him had.

Wouldn't evaporate like the steam from the coffee cup she had ready for him at the counter. Or that he wouldn't walk away before he could get hurt.

Could he hope this time things could be different? His stomach clenched.

He forced himself to let her go.

"Ditto," she said. "I know I say it a lot. But I'm not great with words like you are. Besides, you do describe perfectly the way I feel, and I'm sorry I can't express myself—"

He placed a finger on her lips. "I can see everything I need in your eyes. That's enough for me."

It was taking all his willpower and the reminder that his son was nearby not to kiss her.

Yesterday, he'd hoped she'd go to the patio with him again after tucking in Landon, but she'd disappeared into her room. But then, after four hours of walking on the ship, he couldn't exactly blame her.

All the more, he wanted to make up for the missed kiss now.

He needed to have her in his arms. He needed to taste her lips.

Not just because she made his life easier and brighter.

Or because she made him a better man and parent.

Or because she made the treasure of his life happy.

Not even because he needed to quench that yearning in every fiber of his being.

He just needed her, and that was it.

"Daddy! Hungry here!" Landon's voice brought Kade from fantasyland.

Okay, he wasn't a good father right now. "Hold on, buddy."

He filled their plates and carried them to the table. Then he pulled out her chair. When they were all seated, he reached for their hands and bowed his head.

"I'll say grace!" Landon slipped his tiny hand into Kade's. "Dear Lord, thank You for this food and please bless it. Help Daddy, Auntie H, Grandma, Auntie L, and all my uncles and Dara. Amen. Let's eat."

Kade smiled at the prayer's relative shortness and cut his son's food into smaller pieces.

Then the boy surprised him by bowing his head and whispering, "Lord, I forgot. Please help Daddy see that Auntie H likes him bunches and make him he like her back. I don't wanna her to leave." Looking up, he glanced at his father then at her. "You didn't hear that, right?"

Speechless, Kade just shook his head.

"No," she squeaked as if mortified that her secret was revealed.

So she liked him?

Well, he could guess that much. She wouldn't have kissed him otherwise, and he could feel attraction simmering between them.

But *bunches*? And was there hope for more?

She drained the entire glass of orange juice and cleared her throat. "So, um, what do you want to do today?"

"Go to the beach! Right, Daddy? Auntie H?" Landon was

putting a dent in his breakfast fast as if he couldn't wait to go to the beach.

Hopefully, it wasn't because he expected dolphins to start jumping out of the water like during the aquarium show.

"Sounds great to me." Kade refilled Heather's OJ glass, and touched her hand. "Unless you'd prefer to do something different?"

"No, I'm fine." She smiled. "Let's go to the beach. But we need to make sure to apply sunblock lotion first."

About an hour later, they strolled along the beach.

Well, to be more precise, he and Heather strolled, and Landon and Dara ran forward, dashed back, then ran forward again as if they couldn't understand why the others moved so slowly.

Waves kissed the shore and left soon, only to come back later for another kiss, and seagulls greeted them—or fish. The air would have been hot and humid if the breeze from the ocean hadn't provided a natural air conditioner.

Once they found a good spot, Kade lowered the drink and snack cooler from his shoulder, then set up purple folding chairs and a multicolored umbrella on the sand.

She tucked the large ball and her purse under the umbrella and waved at Landon. "How about we build a sandcastle?"

"Good idea." Kade nodded his approval.

That would keep the boy in one place.

He stole another glance at his wife.

Unlike the tiny, far-too-revealing, bikinis her sister had favored, Heather wore a one-piece dark-blue swimsuit with a flower-patterned skirt and a cerulean-blue sarong wrapped around her hips as if the skirt wasn't modest enough.

Still, she made his breathing shallow and blood rush faster in his veins.

Go figure.

Her long hair flowed from under her cap. They'd worn their

matching caps with puppy patterns and sunglasses again, and it spread warmth inside him, in addition to the warm air. When he'd bought those matching pieces, that was just an idea, wishful thinking for them to become a team.

It was becoming a reality now.

They made some strange constructions they all agreed qualified as sandcastles.

Then Landon leaped to his feet. "Let's play ball."

They formed a small triangle. Heather had told the truth about not being good at sports. She missed catching the ball way more times than she caught it, and she often served it in the wrong direction, but she simply laughed at her mishaps.

She was becoming more comfortable with herself, more accepting of who she was.

Could he hope that one day she'd become more trusting, too?

A little crease on her forehead suggested this wasn't really her thing, but she didn't say a word of complaint.

"We can stop, if you want." He called out to her after sending the ball to Landon.

"No. It's fine. I'm enjoying it."

Respect expanded his chest.

Such a contrast to his ex who'd gone with him on a hike to the lake once, then complained she was tired and had him carry her the entire way. While at first it had been romantic and he'd enjoyed having her close, her constant complaining that the air was too hot, her boots too tight, and her hair frizzing in the humidity had soon worn out his patience.

They'd set up camp and a bonfire near the lake then, and he'd emptied his backpack from meat and soup cans—the food wasn't fancy enough for Josephine, of course. He found himself thinking that at least his backpack would be lighter when they went back and wishing he'd gone on his own.

He frowned as he sent the ball to Landon. Most of his first

marriage he'd spent carrying Josephine's attitude like a heavy burden and wishing he could empty it out of his backpack.

The more time he'd spent with his first wife, the more unpleasant things he'd discovered. Okay, he'd gone into it blinded by infatuation and with high expectations. But while they'd been boyfriend and girlfriend, Josephine had pretended to be sweet and caring.

After the wedding, she didn't have to pretend anymore. The caring persona came off her like her fake lashes.

Hot sand seeping into his flip-flops, he caught the ball from Heather, then sent it to his son.

In this marriage, even in these few days, it was the opposite. He'd gone into it with zero expectations.

No, wrong, he'd gone into it with negative expectations.

Then… he'd loved everything he'd discovered about Heather so far and couldn't wait to discover more. It was as if she'd put up a stern front to keep him—or maybe guys in general—away, and now when he learned more about her, her true beauty blossomed.

Thank You, Lord.

Now, how can I nourish this fragile flower, this delicate attraction growing between us, and not stomp on it and destroy it by accident?

Maybe he was rather shallow and had paid attention to women who'd been only attractive on the outside. By the time he'd started discovering their true characters, he'd already walked away.

Or maybe he'd done that because he knew he wouldn't hurt confident, beautiful women as much when he left. They played the same game and knew the rules.

But this was different.

This wasn't a game.

This shouldn't be short-term.

This had to be real.

In the end, would he be able to stay in this relationship?

Would she?

His rib cage constricted.

"Let's take a break and stay in the shade for a while." He gestured to the umbrella.

Under the umbrella's welcome shadow, he rubbed suntan lotion on his son's exposed arms and legs. He gestured to her suntan lotion in the bag. "Would you like me to—"

"No," she squeaked. "I'm good."

She didn't want him to touch her?

He cringed. "Okay."

Forehead crinkling with disapproval, the boy shook his head. "Auntie H, you're gonna peel. Like an onion."

Her lips curved up. "Like an onion, huh? Well, okay then." She rubbed a bit of the lotion on her arms and legs, then hesitated before reaching her back.

Kade took the tube, squirted some lotion on his palm, and stepped to her. "Let me help you."

Her eyes widened. "I meant… I meant I was going to put it on myself."

"Auntie H, you're not gonna waste it, are you?" The child shook his head again as if he couldn't understand these adults. He settled on the sand under the umbrella and started building sandcastles again.

"I guess not." She visibly swallowed.

As Kade scooted closer and rubbed lotion onto her smooth skin, he pressed his lips tight, and his pulse skyrocketed. It might not have been such a great idea, after all.

Not that he didn't enjoy it—rather, he enjoyed it too much.

Heat pooled in the pit of his stomach. "Is it okay like this?"

"It's great, actually. I think I should do the same for you." Her voice sounded playful.

"Um, okay." In contrast, his voice sounded so husky he barely recognized it.

Was she flirting? Huh. Then she was learning fast.

As he sat in the chair, her light touch was enough to set his blood to surging faster. A rush of heat expanded and engulfed him as if he started swimming in an ocean of desire.

"Like this?" Her voice turned even more playful.

"Yes. Please." His every cell came to life, brimming with pleasure.

How could a simple—even necessary—gesture create euphoria?

When she finished, he turned to her and kept her hands in his. "I think we should visit the beach more often. I didn't realize what I was missing."

"Yeah, Daddy!" His son grinned as he looked up.

"Want a drink, buddy?" Kade walked to the cooler and pulled out a mango juice can and a water bottle.

"Juice, Daddy. Please." The boy darted to him and accepted the can Kade opened for him.

"True. We all need to remember to stay hydrated." Heather accepted the water bottle.

While Landon got busy with sandcastles, she leaned to Kade and whispered as if to make sure the boy wouldn't hear her, "Did your biological father try to contact you again?"

"Hmm." Rather than answer directly, he downed a deep gulp of cold water, grateful for its refreshment. "But I'm sure he will. Maybe my apprehension isn't so much about him, but about myself. He reminds me of who I could become. Who I'd have become if the Clark family hadn't adopted me. He reminds me of things in myself I don't understand or rather don't want to see. Is it ridiculous to still search for identity at thirty-eight? Or maybe it's simply my midlife crisis."

Her gaze became pensive as she unscrewed her water bottle cap. "It's never too early or too late to find oneself. I think you might be worried that he could influence you in a bad way, or more importantly, Landon. But the thing is—you already have core values that I don't think will go away. You have integrity." She paused for a sip.

Her words made him stand taller. "Thank you."

"I blamed you for not paying much attention to me before. But I didn't see much beyond your looks, either. Now I look at you and see a man your son can be proud of. Your family can be proud of. A man I admire." She laid her hand, cold from the bottle, on his chest, then removed it too fast.

"And I'm not just saying this because of your biceps, triceps, and washboard pecs, though those are great, too." Her cheeks pinked.

Wow. She saw him as a better man than he was. But that made him want to be a better man.

"The admiration is mutual." He drained his water bottle, but her words refreshed him even more.

She invigorated him in more senses than one.

"Daddy, let's go to the water." Landon made him look his way. "We gotta see dolphins. We gotta!"

Well, who could resist that logic?

Hours later, Kade drove up to the bungalow, then remembered as he parked. "Would you mind if I get takeout for dinner and buy that dolphin puzzle for Landon?"

"Yay! The puzzle!" The boy clapped from the back seat. "Can I go? Please?"

Kade nodded as he removed the house key from his key chain and handed it to Heather. "Sure."

"Okay. It'll give me time to shower and change." She slid out of the car before he could open her door.

Her phone beeped with an incoming message. She frowned at the screen.

He rolled down the window, her reaction tightening his gut. "Is everything okay?"

"That's from my sister. She says she's closer than we think. Oh no." Her frown deepened. "Giving my father this address was a mistake, wasn't it?"

He searched the street for any cars and found none. "Maybe it's not a good idea for me to leave right now."

He couldn't bear the thought of his ex trying to diminish Heather like she'd done for years. And he wouldn't put it past her to use their son as a bargaining tool again.

"It's okay. I'll be fine." She squared her shoulders and marched to the house.

He loved that change in her, more playfulness, more confidence.

"Daddy, can we go now?" Landon demanded from the back.

Reluctantly, Kade turned on the engine. "Buddy, it'll have to be a fast trip. Very fast."

A thought kept appearing in his mind as he drove off, creating a lump in his throat.

His ex wouldn't show up here, would she?

Chapter Seventeen

"WOW, THAT WAS FAST." Heather ran to the door at the knock. But why would Kade knock? Maybe he had his hands full of groceries?

Dara rose from her place and dashed to the door, barking.

Heather's stomach twisted. It was someone else, not her husband and son. The dog wouldn't be barking at them.

But she didn't know anybody here. She grimaced from a jolt of jealousy as she told the dog to stay. This could be one of Kade's "acquaintances" after hearing he was back in town.

Or…

She glanced in the peephole, and cold traveled down her spine.

Her sister. Argh. Heather would prefer one of those acquaintances.

"Open up, sis. I know you're there."

Frowning, Heather opened the door. "Why are you here?"

"What, no invitation to come in, no sisterly hug?" Josephine barged in, nearly pushing Heather out of the way.

"Sure. Right. Come on in." Heather took a deep breath of expensive perfume as she locked the door and did her best to keep sarcasm out of her voice.

Whatever had happened in the past, she could let it go.

Maybe her sister was just passing through town. Josephine was known for changing locations, men, and opinions often. Hopefully, she'd forgotten her phone threats by now.

Josephine strode into the living room with such confidence as if the place belonged to her and lowered herself onto the sofa. Heather had never noticed before the tiny lines around her eyes or the mean twist of her crimson-smeared mouth.

Heather followed her only sibling and sat on the edge of the chair.

"I came here to get a weekend at the beach and to tell you to stay out of the picture." Using both hands, Josephine gestured as if she were throwing Heather out of the picture already.

Dara stretched on the floor near Heather and growled low as if signaling she'd protect her.

Heather's jaw slackened. "Excuse me?"

As she fluffed her bleach-blonde hair, Josephine looked around. "This is not bad. I'll make sure Kade buys us something like this, only larger. Why are you surprised I'd want to spend a weekend here? They have nice beaches and great seafood, so—"

"No, I'm not surprised about the first part, but the second. About me staying out of the picture."

A sigh lifted Josephine's sculpted shoulders. "You can be so dense sometimes. Despite all the text messages I sent, I have to spell it out. Stay out of the picture, stay out of my way. You have no right to keep my husband and my kid, and it's time I put a stop to it."

She spoke as if Heather had borrowed a designer dress and still hadn't returned it.

Something freezing her in place, Heather gawked at the woman across from her. "You must be kidding me."

One crimson fingernail moved, demarking some point

Josephine was about to make. "I'm not going to let you steal *my* husband and *my* child."

Seconds passed before the words registered.

In the haze, Heather's mind recorded everything else.

A motor growled as a car passed down the street.

Her sister's expensive perfume felt stronger, suffocating, like when they'd been in the public swimming pool on one of the rare out-of-town vacations and her sister—playfully—had pushed her underwater. Like then, Heather struggled for breath as if all the air was sucked from her lungs with a gigantic vacuum cleaner.

She could've drowned that day.

Instead, she'd learned to swim.

The edges of the chair she gripped felt sharp, digging into her palms.

But as soon as she processed the meaning, something inside her roared to life.

Anger, hot as lava, roiled her, exploding to the surface with a surge of scalding words. "*Your* husband? *Your* child? You divorced Kade. You left your child and didn't even bother to call to see how he was doing."

Her sister flipped that long bleached-blonde hair over her shoulder. "I didn't have the time. I was busy. But I'm back now, and I'm going to take what is rightfully mine. And I always— *always*—get what I want." She waited, then added, "Always."

Rising from her chair, Heather planted her hands on her hips. She'd stopped arguing with her sister years ago because it was useless.

This.

Was.

Different.

"Kade and Landon are human beings. You can't leave them and then pick them up whenever you feel like it as if they're playthings on a shelf. They're not your family anymore." She realized something beautiful and amazing amid this turmoil Josephine was creating. "They are mine."

Her sister's heavily mascaraed eyes widened as if she just saw a mouse speak, and she studied her, giving a stare that always made Heather cower and shrink into herself.

This time, Heather straightened her spinal cord to its full capacity and stared back.

Surprise flared the edges of those blue eyes framed by artificial lashes. Then Josephine shrugged. "They are not your family. At least, Landon isn't. You haven't officially adopted him. He's my son by blood and by right. Also, I am your family, and I am telling you to return what you stole from me. Come on, really, what chance do you have?"

Going cold inside, Heather met her stare. She sat again but this time rested against the chair back. "More than you think."

There was the attraction between her and Kade, and Landon loved her, didn't he?

"Oh please. Don't flatter yourself. Dad fessed up how he talked you into proposing to my husband." With a wave of her hand, Josephine laughed. "How ridiculous!"

"Your *ex*-husband," Heather said through her teeth.

Another careless shrug. Another whiff of perfume threatened to suffocate Heather as her sister shifted closer. "Who is soon going to be my husband again. Kade married you for *our* son. Since I'm back, it won't be necessary."

Her stomach tightening, Heather resisted the need to wrap her arms around her middle and rock back and forth like she'd done in her childhood.

Why did her sister have to saunter into their lives and try to ruin everything?

"You never wanted the burden of a family. Why are you doing it now?"

Josephine studied her manicured nails. "Why not?"

As if that was a good enough reason.

As if realizing it, Josephine charged forward. "Okay, maybe I made a mistake leaving Kade. I'm here to correct it. He loved me once. You know that. Everyone in town knows that. I'm the only woman he ever loved."

"Loved. You're his past while I'm his present." How calm she sounded despite the whirlwind of emotions assaulting her.

"Nonsense. I can be very... passionate and tender," her sister practically purred the last words. "It won't take him long to fall in love with me again."

Could this be true?

Heather closed her eyes.

Another car passed in the distance.

Birds chirruped outside.

The refrigerator hummed in the kitchen.

Then there were other sounds in her memory. Kade's laughter when he lifted her in the air, extra pounds and all. His tenderness when he'd said how much she'd meant to him. The murmur of the ocean when he'd kissed her.

Oh, the exhilarating, out-of-this-world feeling of his kiss! She could almost taste his lips against hers again.

Or the decadent deliciousness of the chocolate he'd brought her together with strawberries and caviar. All the things he made her feel, the way he'd made her realize she was worthy of admiration, that he valued and cherished her.

That maybe, just maybe, he and his son needed her as much as she needed them.

She opened her eyes. "I wouldn't be so sure."

Her sister rolled her eyes. "On a one in a million chance, if not, I'm going to take him to court. I'm sure the judge will side with a mother who was deprived of seeing her child for years and suffered so much." Actual tears sheened her sister's eyes. Unreal. "You know I do acting for a living, right? Plus, I have an excellent lawyer to take my case."

How could she and this...actress... be blood-related? "You wouldn't do that."

"You should know me better than to ask." A smile curved those crimson lips, a silent promise in her eyes.

Yes, she did.

Heather's hands fisted. "You'll never win."

"Oh yes, I will. And in the interim, poor Kade and Landon will suffer." The back of her hand flew to her forehead, and she gave out a demonstrative sigh. "All because of you."

"Because of me?" Heather leaped to her feet, anger strengthening her.

Her sister's attractive mouth, enhanced by injections, twisted. "You're the one who doesn't want to remove herself from the equation. Leave before Kade leaves you and let the happy family reunite. Save yourself, Kade, and Landon some suffering."

"How can you do this and look in the mirror at yourself?"

Something flashed in her sister's eyes as she got up, too.

Doubt?

Regret?

It was gone so fast Heather wasn't sure she'd seen it.

"Very easily." Josephine sauntered right in front of Heather. "I'm beautiful and successful while you'll always be living in my shadow."

Heather recalled her husband's words. "I'm beautiful in my own way, with a real, forever kind of beauty while yours is temporary and fake. And I'm much more successful than you realize. I'm successful where it counts to me. But it's not about that now."

"Huh. You changed." Josephine's lashes wobbled as her eyes narrowed. "You changed a lot. But it doesn't matter. I came here to tell you to stay out of my way, and you will if you know what is good for you."

Fortifying herself with a deep breath, Heather rose to her tiptoes so she'd be on the same level with her sister and even felt she grew an inch. "*Try* to move me out of your way. I'll do everything to protect my family. Oh, by the way, I have a lot of pounds on you and a heavy hand."

Josephine lurched back. "You wouldn't dare."

As Heather lifted her fist, Dara got up and growled, drawing closer.

Heather'd never been one for violence and wasn't about to start now, but her sister didn't know that. "I've had enough of this sisterly reunion. Next time you show up here, I'm going to meet you with a skillet and a toaster, and believe me, it's not going to be to make you breakfast."

"What?" the word shrilled past those enhanced lips.

A jolt of satisfaction widened Heather's smile. She did change. "In fact, let me get that skillet right now."

Dara growled again

"I'm going to let myself out." Josephine dashed to the entrance. Once near the door, she stopped, her mouth pursed. "You're going to regret this." She slammed the door behind her.

Heather winced from the sound, her legs wobbling like noodles.

This was only the beginning.

But this time, she wasn't going to hand everything to her sister.

Her sister's words rang in her ears, twisting her gut—*He loved me once, and he's going to love me again. I'm the only woman he ever loved.*

No matter the bond between Heather and her husband, she didn't have the same reassurance, and her heart ached. For herself, for Landon, and for Kade who'd have to make a difficult choice.

Whom would he choose?

CHAPTER EIGHTEEN

AFTER THEY'D TUCKED LANDON in bed and Kade had a long conversation with Heather about his ex's visit, he paced the living room. "I can't believe she'd issue threats like that." He stopped, breathed in, out. "Okay, I know Josephine well enough. I believe it."

His ex's expensive perfume—he knew just how outrageously expensive—lingered in the air, once so familiar, foreign now. It felt like an invasion, nearly as strong as the verbal punch in the face that woman had delivered.

That scent robbed him of air just like she wanted to rob him of his child when it suited her.

He rubbed his temples, headache threatening to move in. "Mind if I open the patio doors?"

"Sure. Go ahead." Heather must be suffocating, too.

He pulled the French doors open, letting in ocean breezes, bringing not just freshness but the memories of their day on the beach, their connection strengthening.

While he was in a mental haze, Dara darted through the opened doors onto the beach.

"Dara, stop!" he yelled, but the dog didn't glance back. If he hadn't been so distraught, he'd have reacted sooner.

"I have to go look for her." He snatched the leash, his mind reeling from his ex's demands. Still wearing his shorts, T-shirt, and sneakers, he sprinted to the shore.

Cool night air met him as he scanned the empty beach.

When Heather fell into step beside him, relief shot through him like adrenaline, though he didn't want Landon to be alone. He slowed as he spotted the dog's massive silhouette against the white sand.

"Dara, here!" he ordered, and Heather joined him.

It would've been helpful to have a dog biscuit or some other kind of treat, but he hadn't had time to get one.

The pet obeyed them this time and rushed to them. Once the dog was close, he clicked the leash locked. "Let's go back."

"We haven't been gone long. I don't think Landon woke up yet, right?"

"I hope not." He wasn't thinking straight when he'd left, and the same concern echoed inside him.

As they approached the bungalow, he stared at the closed patio doors. Huh. "You closed the doors."

Her chin jerked up. "Of course, I did. It's a security measure."

He nodded. "That was the right thing to do. But you took the keys, right? Liberty has one of those locks that lock as soon as you shut the door."

"Oh. Oops." She spread her arms. "I thought you took the keys. Or... I don't know what I was thinking."

His stomach twisted.

He didn't want his son to wake up in the house all by himself and get scared.

"You didn't take the keys. Of course, you didn't." Her palm flew to her mouth. "Oh no. Landon! I am sorry."

As Dara looked from him to her and offered a compassionate whine, Kade squared his shoulders. "It's my fault, too. Mainly my fault. Well, many locksmiths work twenty-four seven." He should know. He used to work for one of them. "We can borrow a neighbor's cell phone to call the service."

"Okay. But while we walk to the neighbor, call the service, while somebody gets here and opens the lock, Landon could get scared."

Dread pooled in the pit of his stomach. Landon's mother had left him once, and the poor child had nightmares for a while.

Waking up in the empty house... That could further damage him.

Kade clenched his jaw and sized up the patio doors. "Maybe I can pry them open. Or..." He didn't finish the sentence.

He didn't want to finish it.

Her eyes pled with him. "Can you try to pick the lock? I mean, at least try? The house belongs to your sister, and once we're inside, I can call her and tell her what happened. In case the police ever question it."

Something moved inside him as if something hidden in the recesses of his mind needed to be pried open again with his bare hands until his hands and his heart bled again.

He'd promised himself he'd never pick a lock again. He'd rather keep it in the past. He was *desperate* to keep it in the past.

But this was about his son.

Kade couldn't let Landon be damaged more than the kid had already been. He couldn't afford to even think about it, couldn't afford to hesitate.

Even if the security alarm went off and he got caught, it was worth the risk. There wasn't even a risk, really, because his sister had given him the house keys.

No risk except in his head.

That silent plea shimmered in Heather's blue eyes. She loved his son nearly as much as he did, and just for that, he'd give up his life for her.

"Heather, do you have a pin?"

Her face lit up. She removed a pin from her shirt.

He started working.

Even after all these years, the rush came in, pumping adrenaline into his blood. He'd missed it. He didn't realize how much.

The lock presented a challenge, a path to the secrets behind the door, to the valuables within his disposal soon. Yes, the treasure was his son, but as more was at stake, the bigger the high was.

His nerve endings came to full alert, and he felt as liquid as an ocean.

He'd experienced the same high when he'd picked locks as a teen. But he'd thought—he'd persuaded himself over the years—that everything was amplified when you were a teen.

One more careful move.

A bit to the left.

Yes, like that.

He thought he couldn't understand why his father had chosen that lifestyle. When the lock clicked and he opened the door, when he reached that new level of high, he understood it too well.

The thought cut him to the core, but he didn't dwell on it. He didn't have time. He rushed inside with Dara, dropped the leash, and disabled the shrieking alarm. Heather was already headed to Landon's room.

The boy met them wide-eyed, sitting on the bed.

Kade hugged his son, Landon's small body trembling, hating himself for letting the alarm scare his child. "It's okay. It's okay. I'm here. You're all right. You're going to be all right."

His gut twisted. No one had held him at night when he'd been a child, nightmares or not.

He shuddered over how it felt to be abandoned, left, discarded. Again and again and again.

Pain and tenderness swirled into one inside him, and he held his boy tighter. "I love you. I love you. I love you."

"Love you, too, Daddy." Landon's voice was so small he barely heard it.

But the words filled Kade with more tenderness, diminishing the pain to a bearable level.

Within minutes, the boy's body stopped trembling, and he eased out of the embrace. "I woke up. I called for you." Then he stretched his hands toward Heather. "You ain't gonna leave me again?"

Huh. The child worried more about Heather's absence than his. Kade was a constant presence in his son's life, while the mother figure—not so much.

He stepped aside.

"Of course not." With a somewhat reassuring and somewhat wobbly smile, she sat on the edge of the bed and hugged his boy.

"Okay." Landon spoke the muffled word into her shoulder.

Then, as she helped him lie back down in bed and stretched the puppy-patterned blanket to his little chest, her smile became less wobbly and more reassuring. "I'm here. See? I'm right here."

The child nodded and then said something that made her eyes widen and breath catch in Kade's throat. "I love you."

She blinked fast as if she tried not to cry, then bent to him and kissed the top of his head. "I love you, too. Very much. Would you like me to tell you a story?"

"Please, pretty please!" His little head bobbled with his enthusiasm.

Kade sat on a small chair that squeaked under his weight as much transfixed by her smooth voice and her kind smile as his child seemed to be. She told a story about the dolphin again.

This time the little fella woke up in the night and was scared. But then his parents showed him the way to the surface where the stars and the moon shone brightly.

Especially one blue shining star.

His heart shifted at the memory of the little blue flower.

Blue shining star.

Once the little dolphin saw that star, he became happy and content and could sleep again.

While she finished, he stepped out of the room to talk to the police that checked on the security alarm going off and had to call his sister to confirm his story.

By the time he returned, Landon's eyes had drooped closed, and his breathing had evened out.

After Kade and Heather tiptoed out of the boy's room, he placed a kiss on her cheek, holding her longer than necessary as if he, like his son, needed to know she wouldn't be going away soon. "Thank you. Thank you so much for everything."

"You don't have to thank me. When I said I loved your son, I meant it." She yielded into his arms, fitting into his embrace as if she were made for him.

Excitement rushed his blood faster in his veins, so he disentangled himself from her. A man could only have so much willpower. She still insisted on separate bedrooms, and he wouldn't push her if she wasn't ready, married or not.

Besides, there were things he needed to think about. "Good night, my darling wife. Sleep well."

Disappointment flashed in her eyes. She hesitated as if she were going to say something, giving him hope.

For what, he wasn't sure.

Then she looked down. "Good night."

She slipped behind the door, and he stared at it. There was no lock on that door, which didn't matter because, if there was, it wouldn't be one even he could pick.

He started feeling close to her, so close.

Yet, there was still a door between them.

He walked to Dara who'd waited in the hall, behaving like an ideal dog now, took her from her leash, washed her paws, and gave her fresh water and a biscuit.

Then he stood near the patio window and gazed at the ocean, empty inside. When one of the older kids in a foster home had taught him how to pick a lock, he'd said Kade had talent.

You're a born thief.

His biological father had said the same thing.

His stomach clenched.

Then there had been his time of self-searching at twenty-five, and he'd wanted so badly to know where he'd come from, people he'd come from that he'd agreed to spend the time with his biological dad, give him a chance to right the wrong.

That guy had told him he'd taken after him—after Kade had passed all his lessons smoothly. Kade had been scared to look inside himself ever since.

He frowned. Of all the talents in the world, he had to get that one. He couldn't explain why he had the rush, the craving.

Thanks to God, he was well-off now. He didn't have his biological father's excuse that he'd needed to feed his child. No explanation—other than this was in his blood.

At the light footsteps, he turned around.

Heather, adorable in her puppy pajamas, approached, worry in her eyes.

She knew.

The thought flashed like lightning and sizzled away, but it illuminated the truth already.

She knew who he was inside.

The next thought rumbled like thunder.

Did it scare her as much as it scared him?

"It's okay. You did what you needed to do," she whispered.

"I craved it. That unthinkable desire was inside me. My biological father once said some people are born to become doctors. Some are born to become ranchers. And some are born to be thieves or con artists. Because otherwise why would we be so good at it?" He winced at his use of the word *we*.

He already identified himself with that guy.

Son, that's where you come from. You might as well accept it. They put different things in your head, but the truth is you're just like me. This is in your blood—nothing you can do about it. If to be a thief, then to be a great one. If to be a con artist, then to be a great one. I can tell, you have the potential to be great.

A lightning bolt split the sky outside.

Then thunder nearly deafened him, and rain followed.

Dara gave a low whine but stayed in her place on the living room floor.

He listened, afraid the thunder would wake his son. No, everything was quiet behind that door.

"It didn't even smell like rain before. Things happen when we least expect them," he said quietly.

She padded to his side and hugged him. Then there was nothing besides the sounds of their breathing and the rain pounding on the roof. He listened again for any distress from the kid's room, but none came, so he relaxed a little.

Something shifted within him from her embrace. Still, he couldn't let it go. "They say a leopard doesn't change his spots. Maybe what happened tonight confirms it. "

"Listen to me, please." Her whisper heated on his skin. "You are a wonderful person. Your heritage doesn't define you. Your youthful mistakes don't define you. I know it all affected you, but look how far you've come. It's not about what you're given, but about what you do with it."

The words clicked, like a lock that finally opened.

He said them again and again, as if it could help him find the path to himself again.

It's not about what you're given, but about what you do with it.

She rose on her tiptoes and hugged him tighter.

"It's going to be all right. It's going to be okay," she repeated the words he'd told his son, but they didn't offend him, didn't make him feel like a little boy.

Instead, they soothed the rough edges.

Maybe she was saying all this because she was kindhearted and sweet, but he didn't care. He had to believe all she said was truth.

She moved back, and their gazes met and held again. "It's not about the family we're born into. It's about the family we choose—or rather God gives us along our path—and we accept, if we're wise enough to see it."

The family we choose...

"I didn't choose you, I know, but I'm grateful God made that choice for me." He drank in her sweet expression, the sincerity and admiration in her blue eyes, despite all she knew about him now. "That you had enough courage to propose. Knowing you better now, I realized how difficult it must've been. It's even more amazing that you accept me the way I am, with all the broken pieces and doubts you now know about."

She gave him a quick squeeze. "There's nothing wrong with you, inherently or otherwise. You're your own person and one of the greatest gifts from God I've ever had."

"And you are mine. I just wish you accepted yourself the way you are, too. That you loved yourself and cared about yourself with the same abandonment as you care about others."

She nodded. "Thanks to you, I'm learning to. Look into my eyes."

"I do. They are beautiful. You're beautiful." He meant every word.

"Um, thank you, but that's not what I meant. Can you see your reflection in my eyes? Can you see the man I see?" She brought herself closer as if to help him see his reflection in her blue orbs.

"What man is that?"

Her pink lips curved up. "A good-hearted man who works hard and does everything he can for the people he loves. You even want to help teens who are in the situation you were. You could've chosen a life with no responsibilities, just coasting on your family's wealth, but you didn't. You have honesty and integrity, or you wouldn't be struggling like you struggle right now. You talk about God often, so try to see yourself the way God created you."

He hugged her like he never wanted to let her go.

Because he didn't. "I needed this. I need to hold onto this. Onto you. Besides Landon, you're something solid in my life."

A nervous giggle burst from her. "Yeah, I'm solid. Well, some parts of me are wobblier than others."

"Stop it. Every inch of you is perfect."

Her eyes widened. "Do you really think so?"

"I do."

Then she did something he didn't expect, considering her shyness. She found his lips and kissed him.

He became fluid like the ocean again, but on a different level, something higher, more incredible, and less comprehensible. Every cell in his body shimmered with delight. He got lost in the kiss, the pleasant sensations, the sweet scent of her hair, and the knowledge that this meant something, that it meant a lot.

That his life was never going to be the same.

That he was never going to be the same.

If there was a cleansing quality to the kiss, this was it.

When they both came up for air and he let her go, he looked at her as at the miracle she was. And now he had a different kind of craving.

He hid his face in her hair, breathed in her flowery perfume, then let it go because he needed to see her eyes. "I need you. Oh, how much I need you. You're so good to me. Why are you so good to me?"

"Because I love you." Her hand flew to her mouth as if she'd said too much.

He let it sink in.

She was an even bigger miracle than he'd thought.

A gift he didn't expect and didn't deserve.

While euphoria filled him at her confession, doubt wormed through it, too. He'd messed up all his romantic relationships.

How was he to hold onto this precious gift and not break it?

He didn't reply with "I love you, too," because he wasn't absolutely sure. He felt strongly about her, very strongly, but he couldn't say the words. Pain knifed him at the disappointment in her expression. He was breaking that gift already, hurting her already.

More words that his biological father had told him filtered through his mind.

People like us aren't meant to stay with one woman. It's not in our DNA. If we try, we hurt them in the end. I did several times, and it never ended well.

The rain stopped. There was no more thunderstorm or lightning.

In the sudden silence, her words sounded louder in his head, repeated again and again.

I love you.

I love you.

I love you.

His phone rang from the desk where he'd left it, and he cringed.

"It might be something important." She eased away.

He glanced at the screen and sucked in a sharp breath.

His brother. Mac wouldn't call this late unless there was an emergency. Could something have happened to one of the Thoroughbreds?

Or even worse.

His gut twisted as he swiped the screen to answer. "What happened?"

"I'm sorry to call late and also to interrupt your vacation. But I thought you needed to know. Your house was burglarized."

Pent-up air whooshed out of Kade's lungs. That wasn't so bad. But it meant they might need to cut their vacation short. "Thank you for letting me know."

"The strange part, it doesn't look like the lock was tampered with."

CHAPTER NINETEEN

THE NEXT DAY, Kade resisted the urge to grind his teeth as he investigated the empty rooms. He'd left Landon at his mother's place at her request and to spare the kid the unpleasant surprise. Besides, Grandma couldn't wait to see her darling grandson.

"All the electronics are gone. Some furniture, too. I'm so sorry." Why'd Heather sound apologetic? It wasn't her fault.

"It's okay." On his phone, he listed the stolen things for the police as he moved through the rooms.

They'd stopped by the police department on the way and were told not to touch anything but make a list of the things missing. Then they'd left the dog and Landon with his grandmother. "It all can be replaced."

But more important things, like trust, couldn't be replaced.

A crazy thought intruded in his mind—more intuition? He shook his head.

No, this was too farfetched.

He texted his biological father.

YOU WOULDN'T HAPPEN TO KNOW ANYTHING ABOUT THE BURGLARY, WOULD YOU?

The reply came back quickly.

GREAT GUESS. I NEEDED STARTUP CAPITAL, AND YOU WEREN'T THERE, SO I COULDN'T BORROW IN PERSON. TECHNICALLY, YOUR FAULT I HAD TO RESORT TO THIS. CONSIDER IT A LOAN. YOU WOULDN'T MIND, WOULD YOU?

Kade gawked at the screen.

The guy never changed.

That meant Kade could never change, either.

Some things were in his blood.

He needed time to process this.

Maybe time to find his biological father and retrieve what he'd taken.

Then another crazy idea assailed him. An idea that could save them all some suffering. "Would you mind if we spent a few days apart? We won't tell Landon, of course. I need to regroup and… do some things. And once Josephine gets wind of us being apart, she'll lose interest and leave. She only wants me and Landon now because she can't have us."

He regretted his words as soon as he said them.

His stomach twisted at the hurt in her eyes.

"I should've known this wouldn't last. I should've known!" After stamping her foot as if she'd reverted to the little girl who'd been hurt so many times, she turned and fled.

"Wait! I didn't mean that—Let me explain!" He ran after her, tripped over an overturned chair, and hit the floor face-first.

Pain exploded inside him, but he scrambled to his feet as fast as he could.

By the time he ran outside, her car was gone.

Another car, a luxurious one, parked at the curb, and his ex slid out of it with her usual gracefulness. "Oh, how sad. I saw tears in my sister's eyes. But then, what did you expect? Your affections never lasted."

"It's not what you think." Resisting the urge to grind his teeth, he pivoted around her.

Josephine sauntered toward him, all smiles. "You told her you needed to spend some time apart. All that it's-me-not-you speech."

How hadn't he seen how fake she was? He jumped inside his truck. "Yes, but—"

"That's what you usually say," she sing-songed.

Was it?

He scolded himself as he started the engine.

How could he?

He read Josephine's lips rather than heard her next words. How could he ever have found her smug smile so attractive. "Heather isn't like me. She'll never forgive you."

A shiver traveling down his spine, he drove off, peeling rubber.

He'd just made the biggest mistake of his life.

Kade's heart sank as he returned to his truck after knocking on Heather's door.

As he'd made the statement at the police station, her words kept appearing in his head.

It's not about what we're given. It's what we do with it.

It's not about the family we're born into. It's about the family we choose, or rather God gives us along our paths and we accept, if we're wise enough to see it.

There's nothing wrong with you, inherently or otherwise. You're one of the greatest gifts from God I've ever had.

After giving the statement, he slipped into the driver's seat at the police station parking lot. The realization of what he'd done hit, and he slapped the steering wheel.

But it wasn't the truck's fault that he couldn't see what was right in front of his eyes.

Why couldn't he see it?

Heather was his gift from God, one of the biggest ones he'd ever received. The family God had given him along the way.

The amazing person who'd stick with him through thick and thin if he hadn't messed it up. His stomach clenched as he turned the key in the ignition and the motor revved to life.

He'd said once that he wished she'd see herself the way he saw her, but maybe indeed he was the one who needed to see himself through her eyes because she'd seen him in a mighty better light than he'd seen himself. And she'd seen him whole, not broken, not someone with bad genetics or a heritage leaving a lot to be desired.

She'd seen him as someone worthy of love.

He must've had a moment of temporary insanity when he'd asked her to leave.

Now, when she was gone, he had a deep, painful void. He missed seeing her beautiful eyes, feeling her kindness toward him and his son in every gesture, even hearing her nervous giggles and self-deprecating humor.

But most of all, he missed the feeling he'd had these last days.

He was happy. Completely, deliriously happy.

More importantly, his son was happy. Kade couldn't even think of the effect this could have on Landon.

The void seemed to grow, making it harder to breathe.

What had he done? How could he ask her to leave, even if for a few days?

He drove from the parking place, no doubt in his mind.

He loved her.

It wasn't gratitude, infatuation, mutual respect, though there was all that, too.

He loved her.

He missed her. He needed her. He wanted to spend the rest of his life with her.

Lord, thank You for this clarity.

As Kade drove, he called her on the hands-free phone, but she didn't answer.

His heart sinking, he left a message, "I'm sorry. I'm so very sorry. Please call me back." There was so much more he wanted to say, but he wanted to say it in person.

His heart squeezed.

Where could she be?

An incoming call on the hands-free phone made him perk up, but he grimaced as his sister's number appeared on the screen. "Hello, sis."

"I'd get upset at that lukewarm greeting if I didn't want to kill you already." Liberty never wasted time on pleasantries. No surprise there. "How could you do this to Heather?"

"I made a mistake. The biggest mistake of my life." That was a statement, considering he'd made many mistakes in his life. "But I'm trying to correct it. She is not at home. Is she at your place?"

"Negative to both. She called me but said she wanted to be alone. Of course, I bought a box of chocolate-covered donuts and went to her place. She wasn't there. Her phone isn't answering now."

His heart sank lower. "If you find her, or if she calls you, please let me know."

"You, too." Worry tightened his sister's voice. "I'm going back to my place, in case she decided to stop by. When we were teens, she said our library was her favorite place in the world. Oh, check the ice-cream parlor. She loved visiting it, too."

"Yes. Thanks. I'll also call her father and check other places in town."

"Don't thank me. I'm going to smack you upside down when we meet. Too busy for it now." His sister disconnected.

His heart ached more and more with every passing minute.

He stopped at the ice-cream parlor and talked to people there, then returned to the truck and started making calls.

192

Her parents didn't know where she was, and neither did anyone he called in town, including the biggest gossip who could track down the movements of their small town residents better than an ankle bracelet.

He knew better than to call Josephine.

Liberty phoned and told him Heather didn't show up at her place, either.

A shiver moved down his spine after he checked the restaurants, bakery, and pretty much every eating establishment in town and even talked to the gas station attendant.

After Kade returned to her place and talked to her neighbors, all to no avail, dread pooled in the pit of his stomach.

What happened to her?

A tentative hope filled him as he stopped near the park, and he raced to the hiking trail he'd taken her on. Taking deep breaths of fresh air, he found the bench where he'd carved their names and ran his fingertips over the uneven surface.

Empty.

She wasn't here.

Disappointment cut deep, cutting even deeper when he saw no blue shining stars. The flowers were gone.

Heather was gone.

His phone rang. His heart jumped as he glanced at the screen. Then his heart dipped again.

Mac.

Kade swept his screen to answer. "If it's about work, I'm sorry, I'm busy right now."

"I know. I heard what happened. I'm searching for Heather, too."

"Thanks." He winced as guilt over his outburst stabbed at him.

"No need to thank me. We're family. We stay together."

Kade swallowed around the lump in his throat as he walked back to his truck. "Yeah. I forgot that important rule when I asked

Heather to stay away for a few days."

"Everyone makes mistakes. It's okay." Mac's voice grew stronger, just like his handshakes or back pats that were close to sending Kade launching forward. "We're going to find her."

"Thanks, bro." The weight of his error pressed on his shoulders as he slid inside the truck and turned the key in the ignition again.

"We're going to find her," Mac repeated. "We have several prayer chains started already. Soon the entire town will be looking for her. She's more loved than she realizes, and you know you're popular here. No stone will be left unturned."

Breath caught in his throat as he drove off.

He'd been stupid to look for something else.

This town, these people were his family.

Despite his questionable past, they'd accepted him. They cared about him. They loved him unconditionally.

Just like Heather had.

"I'm going to park near her house for some time. Maybe she'll show up."

"I'll keep in touch and will keep you posted." His brother disconnected.

As Kade made a turn, his rib cage constricted.

Did she drive somewhere where that guy could land a private jet and whisk her away? The lump in his throat grew. Despite a sharp stab of jealousy, that was a better version than the alternative.

That something happened to her.

All because of him.

He sent up his most fervent prayer ever. *Lord, please keep Heather safe in Your care. Please let us find her. Amen.*

CHAPTER TWENTY

HEATHER DROVE FOR A WHILE without knowing where she was going. She'd stopped at her place, but without Landon's laughter, Dara's barking, and Kade's voice, it was too quiet.

She'd left her bag at her husband's—probably a husband for not much longer—so she'd packed the few clothes she'd had left and rushed to her car again.

Her phone rang, but she let it go to voice mail as she drove.

She loved Kade enough to give him freedom.

But how was she going to live without him and the nephew she adored as her own son?

Tears burned behind her eyes, and she blinked fast to prevent them from spilling. Her fingers tightened around the steering wheel as she made a sharp turn.

Tires squealed.

She drew a deep breath and eased up on the gas pedal. She'd always been a careful driver.

After that one time, she'd also been careful not to fall in love, to guard her fragile heart.

Too late for that now. She rolled down the window because it was hard to breathe, so hard to breathe, and the air conditioner wasn't enough.

She realized where she was going. Was she driving to the lake?

Its peaceful image brought back now-painful memories.

Lord, are You listening? Why is this happening? What's wrong with me?

There was nothing wrong with her.

The answer appeared in her mind almost immediately.

But nothing else.

Every fiber of her hurting inside, she stopped the engine and ran to the lake.

She changed into a swimming suit and entered the water—not a good idea to swim in the lake, but she didn't care.

As she stepped into the water, she could see the sand on the bottom of it.

And then she started seeing other things, inside herself. She could recover from this.

She wasn't ready to give up on her family yet, give up on her chance to be with Kade, to be a mother to his son. She was going to return and talk to him, again and again.

Her heart squeezed, and she braced for cool water as she started swimming. If all his words were empty compliments he hadn't meant, if he still decided to call it quits…

Well, she'd move forward then.

She'd live her life and maybe meet a man God meant for her when the time was right. She finally learned to appreciate herself the way she was.

She'd always concentrated on her extra pounds instead of her mind or the good qualities of her character. She was worthy of love and admiration of others, but she'd needed to love and admire herself first. Maybe all these years, people had seen her in a negative way because she'd seen herself that way.

Lord, thank You for helping me understand this.

She'd thought that she was born to be fat.

Instead, she was born to be happy.

With each stroke, the water seemed to cleanse her from her hang-ups. In the interim, she'd love herself the way she was, accept herself the way she was, and be happy.

It was going to take a while, and a few tears dropped into the water, followed by a sob. But she was going to get there.

About half an hour later, Kade let his head drop on his arms on the steering wheel. He'd already called Heather a million times, but her phone wasn't answering at all.

Liberty and Mac called, but they had no news.

The search had yielded zero results so far.

Kade had even swallowed his pride and managed—with great difficulty—to track down and talk to Stewart Del Bosque. He hadn't heard from Heather, either.

Kade's heart was crushing into pieces. And this was going to break Landon's little heart. He'd talked to his son several times on the phone, doing his best to sound cheerful. Somehow, the family managed to keep Heather's disappearance from the boy. They wouldn't be able to do it forever.

Heather was a responsible, sensible woman. She... she wouldn't hurt herself, would she?

Kade shuddered.

He didn't know what to do next.

So he did the only thing he could.

He stared ahead of him at the blue sky and prayed.

Lord, please forgive me. Please give me another chance with Heather. Please help me find her.

For a few moments, nothing happened.

Then an image of the lake appeared

The lake. Why the lake?

Confusion clouded his mind even more, when it already wasn't in good shape.

Oooooh.

Maybe Heather could've gone to the lake where all three of them had been so happy. He started the engine and drove off fast.

The chance was small, but he had to check it.

So he floored the gas pedal, the motor roaring in his ears. He called Liberty on the hands-free and let her know where he was going.

Soon he parked near the lake, turned off the engine, and rushed outside.

Hope expanded his chest at the sight of her blue-flowered dress fluttering on the dock railing. He studied the lake's mirrored surface, and hope dissipated fast. He couldn't see her.

Why couldn't he see her?

Dread replaced hope.

No, no, no.

She couldn't have drowned. She'd said she was a good swimmer, hadn't she?

A motor made him look back. Tires squealed as his sister's hunter-green vehicle came to a complete stop.

Liberty jumped out of the truck. "Did you find her?"

He gestured to the dress.

Her eyes widened. "Oh no. She couldn't have drowned. She's a great swimmer. Unless—"

She didn't finish the sentence, maybe because, like him, she didn't want to put the terrifying thought into words.

That Heather could drown *on purpose.*

"I'm going to check the lake." He took off his T-shirt and kicked off his shoes as determination filled him.

"Hello!" Liberty lifted her hand in the universal sign of stop. "You're not a good swimmer."

"Neither are you."

"Why don't you wait? Soon more people will be here."

"I don't want to wait. I can't wait." He ran toward the water.

"Kade, no!" His sister's voice hit him in the back, but he didn't stop.

He didn't linger to test the water but plunged forward as cool water met him.

Worry constricting his lungs, he swam forward. He could do well enough to stay on the surface, right?

After a few strokes, he could see her. He could see her head, her face above the water. Joy filled everything in him.

She was alive.

She was okay.

Even if she never gave him a chance again, he thanked God a million times that she was fine.

"Heather!" he yelled and tried to wave.

Her head turned as if she'd spotted him, too, and he nearly went numb at the thought she might turn around and swim in another direction.

She didn't. She swam toward him.

His chest expanded.

"I'm sorry!" He screamed louder because he couldn't wait to tell her.

Maybe he should've waited because water flooded in his mouth, and he started coughing. At the same time, a muscle in his leg spasmed.

No.

No.

No.

The seizure made him gasp for air with greediness, but he only got more water into his lungs.

Suddenly, he felt heavy, so heavy as if he became filled with lead and the water couldn't keep him on the surface any longer. He shuddered and went underwater as pain from his leg ricocheted through his entire body.

He couldn't breathe.

His arms flailed while his lungs begged for oxygen. He was as hungry for air as he was to tell Heather he loved her.

Would he have a chance to tell her now? He… he couldn't leave Landon.

Not like this.

Not now.

Terror filled Kade's brain even as he felt pulled down, deeper and deeper and deeper, despite his flailing limbs. He should have more strength than this.

He should!

His mind was becoming foggier and his movements more erratic. The ringing in his ears intensified.

Lord, please help me. And if something happens to me, please take care of my family. Amen.

Somehow, he couldn't think straight, couldn't name them all.

Then something—somebody—started pulling him up.

Arms.

Somebody's arms.

The dark one-piece swimming suit.

Long hair.

Heather!

He moved his legs and arms as much as he could until he breached the surface and gasped for air.

More air.

More!

He wanted to tell her so much but was afraid he'd sink again if he opened his mouth.

"You scared me so much. Why would you try this when you don't swim well?" She helped him stay on the surface, so much worry in her beautiful eyes.

"I–I wanted to save you from drowning. I thought you were... upset, and..." He didn't sound too cohesive, did he?

"Why would I drown? I just needed some time to myself. But... it's better for you to stop talking, I think."

He needed to say this as they were trying to swim to the shore. Well, it was more her directing him and him doing his best not to go underwater again. "I love you. I love you. I love you so much. I love you. Don't leave. Don't ever leave me."

Her face lit up, but concern settled in her eyes again. "I heard you the first time. I'm here. I'm not going anywhere."

She was here.

She was here.

She was here.

Thank You, Lord! Thank You so much!

Despite the circumstances, euphoria buoyed him.

By the time they reached the part of the lake where he could feel the sandy bottom, Mac was already there and dragged him out as he placed Kade's arm over his shoulder. "What were you thinking? I'm going to kill you."

"Get in line." Kade's insides trembled.

"I called the ambulance. They should be here any moment." Liberty ran to them with towels and blankets. "Tomorrow, I'll be shopping for life jackets for everyone in the family."

Without enough strength left to dry out, he collapsed onto the grass. "I don't need an ambulance."

"Not negotiable." Liberty covered him with a blanket while she handed the rest to Mac and Heather.

The welcome warmth didn't stop Kade's shivering, though. His whole body shaking, he searched his wife's gaze.

"I'm going to be okay." He infused his voice with reassurance. "Heather, please forgive me. I don't want to spend a day apart from you. I don't want to spend a moment apart from you. I need you. I need you like air." He coughed.

"I think right now you need air more." The corners of her lips curved up. "You shouldn't be talking."

Yeah, he needed to show her instead of talking.

Show her he was in this marriage for life.

Show her he meant every word.

Show her how much she meant to him.

Kinda ridiculous and silly to do this now, but he couldn't wait another moment.

As he winced at a siren's distant shrill, he looked around from his vantage point on the grass. "Does anyone have something circular?"

Liberty blinked and elbowed Mac. "I think he stayed without oxygen for too long," she whispered loud enough for everyone to hear.

"I didn't pass out, and I'm thinking clearly." Well, more or less. Kade still had ringing in his ears, and his limbs felt weak. But he needed to do this. Heather had to know. "Please?"

"Okay, I've got chocolate-covered donuts." Liberty turned as if to run to her vehicle.

Heather leaned to him, so much love and concern in her baby blues, his blue shining stars. "What are you trying to do? The ambulance will be here soon. You'll be okay. You have to be okay."

"I have something to ask you. Something important." He stared in her luminous eyes, then stopped his sister with a gesture when she handed him a donut box. "That's too big. Something smaller?"

His brother hesitated. "I've got mini-donuts I bought for my daughter."

Not even close.

But it would have to do.

Kade nodded. "Please bring them."

While his brother headed to his vehicle and returned, Kade

wobbled to lift himself enough to get on one knee. Thankfully, one could do this on one knee instead of standing up.

There was a collective gasp.

"Oh, I get it." With a smile, his brother handed him a powder-sugar-covered donut.

The ambulance screeched to a halt, and two paramedics approached with a stretcher.

"What happened here?" the male paramedic demanded on the way.

The female paramedic shook her head and sent him a "hush" glance.

Good. Kade had a few seconds.

"Heather, I know it's not a real ring and we're already married. But I need to do this because I can't bear even the thought of losing you again. I want you to know I love you with my whole heart. Well, you and Landon."

She chuckled as tears filled her eyes. "You really—"

"Will you make me the happiest man alive? No, that's wrong."

Another collective gasp spread through the group.

"Wrong?" Heather squeaked.

"I mean, you already made me the happiest man alive. I want to do the same for you in return for as long as I live. And I want you to know our marriage is real, very real."

The male paramedic snorted. "With a mini-donut?"

"For some people, it's worth more than a diamond ring," the female paramedic hissed at him. "And I'm sure he'll replace it with a diamond ring later. You should be taking notes."

"Sorry, have my hands too busy with a stretcher for that."

These two would probably be married someday.

Kade refocused on his wife. "I mean, I know about the mistakes in my youth and that I don't have good genetics—"

The female paramedic coughed. "*He* says he doesn't have

good genetics? I mean, look at him!"

This time the male paramedic sent his colleague a "hush" glance.

"I love you, too. Very much. That's why I was going to give you freedom if you asked for it. But if you want to stay married to me… the answer is—yes, yes, and yes." Heather beamed while he slid the mini-donut on her finger and covered his face in kisses.

Everybody clapped except the male paramedic. "We've got a job to do here, people!"

Just as his heart sang from happiness, Kade still needed to make sure. "You didn't say yes because you want to get me inside the ambulance as soon as possible?"

The male paramedic groaned. "That's enough. Let me check your vital signs. Let's get going. Oh, and we'd better get a wedding invitation."

The girl sighed as she checked Kade's blood pressure. "Deep down, my colleague is a romantic at heart. Uh-oh. Your blood pressure is rather high."

As worry reflected on Heather's face, he squeezed her hand. "I'm just excited to be married again."

"Again?" the girl asked as she fitted him with an oxygen mask.

"The first time resulted in divorce. And the second time he was rather reluctant to get married," Liberty explained as she walked near the stretcher on one side while Heather walked on the other side.

"Spare me the details." The guy shook his head.

That romantic thing must be very *deep* down.

Kade wanted to say this one was going to be the only marriage for him, but he couldn't with the oxygen mask on.

Neither could he kiss his wife.

He made a heart sign with his hands the best he could, hoping she'd understand him.

She did.

She smiled at him, a happy gleam in her eyes slightly clouded with worry. "I love you, too. Very much so."

He could look forward to a lifetime of this.

A week later, Heather laughed as Landon hugged his toy dolphin and announced, "It's gonna be the bestest day ever!"

"Find your cap. We're leaving for the children's museum in minutes." Kade ruffled his son's hair, then put his own cap on and winked at her while his son disappeared in his room. "He's right, you know. With you, every day is the bestest day ever."

As a pleasant wave spread inside her, she snugged the matching cap over her hair. They'd bought ones with a dolphin pattern for everyone this time. And she didn't wave off his compliment as she used to.

Instead, she cuddled against him when he hugged her. "Ditto."

She was a different person now, much more confident than before.

The house looked different now, too.

Over the weekend, they'd bought new furniture and electronics and even brought over her favorite antique pieces from her house which she'd put up for sale. She'd liked his house before, but it looked more like her home now.

And they'd added a painting with the dolphins Landon loved so much.

The quick kiss Kade planted on her cheek still managed to give her butterflies in her tummy. "I'm falling more and more in love with you every day. It's going to be dangerous to my blood pressure when I turn eighty."

She laughed again. She'd laughed more with him in two weeks than she had in her entire lifetime before.

All forty years of waiting for this incredible man.

Still, some habits lingered. "How come an outrageously handsome player like you fell in love with a chunky, quiet introvert like me?"

Okay, maybe she wasn't that insecure anymore.

But she liked to hear his compliments, and so far, he kept them coming, as well as caviar, bouquets of white roses, and lots and lots of chocolate.

He looked into her eyes, admiration shining in his. "First of all, like I said, every inch of you is beautiful. Second, I remember the software projects you told me you developed. I researched some of them online. Wow."

"Well, it wasn't that—"

"Seriously, wow. I have a brilliant wife. While players like me partied and went from one relationship to another, quiet introverts like you changed the world. Third, I love you because you're amazing. Fourth—"

"Daddy, I'm ready!" Landon charged into the room.

As they walked to the truck, the boy's hand in his, she nudged Kade. "If Landon didn't interrupt us, how many points did you have on this list?"

"Two hundred seventy-five. I'm working on more." He winked at her again as he clicked the truck open.

"Mommy, Daddy, can we stop for ice cream?" Landon asked as Kade hefted him into the harnessed booster seat.

For a moment, the world stood still. It seemed neither Kade nor she could find their tongue.

Mommy.

Was it too soon?

Should she say something?

Happy tears prickled in the back of her eyes.

Kade hugged her and kissed her, sending more butterflies dancing in her stomach. "Congratulations! I couldn't be happier," he whispered into her ear, his breath hot on her skin.

Forget eighties.

He was dangerous to her blood pressure now, based on how erratic her heartbeat became.

Her breath lodged in her throat.

"Well, can we? Pretty, pretty please?" The boy's voice jolted her from her stupor.

"Of course, we can, buddy." Kade opened the door for her.

They drove in silence as she tried to process the moment's significance.

"I'm so grateful your son accepted me like this," she whispered to Kade.

"Our son." He smiled at her before returning his attention to the road.

Remembering yesterday's text, she shifted to Kade. "I probably shouldn't say it, but I'm glad my sister left the same day you saw her near our house. Did I mention that she said she met a guy, quite a bit older than she is? He was loaded and charming, so she didn't mind the age gap."

He glanced at her, a strange look in his eyes as they made a turn. "Huh. It's a crazy thought, but you wouldn't think my father and she…"

"Nah. That would be too much of a coincidence." She reached for his hand.

She was so deliriously happy she'd forgiven her sister all she'd put her through. And Heather finally loved herself the way she was.

Thank You, Lord.

Her heart swelled. She even found her way to God and became grateful for the way He created her.

She glanced back at a grinning Landon—her son, even if the adoption papers she'd filed were going to take a while—then smiled as her husband's fingers tightened around hers.

It was about time for her to learn to look forward to every day, the bestest day ever.

EPILOGUE

A month later.

THE VOW RENEWAL and then the outside lakeside reception while sunlight basked the water in a soft glow tugged the heartstrings of even a pragmatist like Mac.

A light breeze touched his face, bringing freshness and scents of Cowboy Crossings scattered on the grass. The latter were the courtesy of the prettiest flower girl ever who took her duties so seriously that she was still running around and spreading petals.

He might be a tad biased because his daughter was the flower girl. Dressed in a light-blue dress with a ridiculous amount of bows and tiny matching shoes, she made his heart expand. How could her mother choose alcohol addiction over this treasure?

He'd never know, and the woman hadn't been around for years to ask.

His gut twisted, but he made sure the turmoil didn't reflect on his face as his daughter ran up to him. "All done, Daddy."

He lifted her into a nearby chair where a plate of her favorite snacks already waited for her. "Great job, darling. Great job."

If there was a second marriage, a second chance for his

younger brother, could there be a second one for him, too?

Something prickled behind Mac's eyes, and he bent to his daughter, breathed in the sweet papaya scent of her favorite shampoo, partly because that scent and the kiss on her soft curls never failed to fill him with tenderness.

And partly because he needed to hide his moment's weakness.

When he looked up and nodded to Kade, who was pouring apple cider for his wife, that weakness was gone.

Mac was fine with his life, really, raising his child and having a job he loved.

The family ranch was doing better than he could wish for. He finally had peace after years of scandals and broken dishes. He could sleep through the night instead of staying up worrying and waiting for unsure steps in the hall. Then, when none came, dragging his drunken wife home from the house of her best friend who harbored the same affection for whiskey, her slurred speech and whiskey-stained breath leaving him nauseated.

His heart constricted as he filled her daughter's glass with her favorite lemonade.

He truly knew how to choose them, didn't he? His first love had left town after the best summer of his life, never to return or even contact him. His second did the same, though after the two most miserable years of his life.

He uncoiled his fingers as he tried to push a bite past the lump in his throat. He didn't even realize when his hand had fisted.

He smiled at Kade and his wife, who despite half the town being guests at the renewal ceremony, seemed to have eyes only for each other. Well, and their boy, of course.

Landon ran to them. "Mommy, look at the dolphin Auntie L gave me." He showed her the new toy.

"It's a great dolphin." Heather hugged the boy, happy tears in her eyes.

The child was calling her "Mommy" now, and Mac wasn't

surprised. She'd showered the kid with an ocean of love for years, an ocean more than Landon's biological mother ever had.

Huh.

Mac drank some of his apple cider.

Some women left their children, and some were happy to raise their nephew with a love no one ever expected from them. Even a bigger miracle was that his youngest brother had settled down and realized what was good for him.

Mac had never seen so much happiness shine in Kade's eyes, and his wife was luminous.

She wore the same simple white dress she'd worn to the wedding, and her hair was swept in the same way with wildflowers woven in. His younger brother wore the same tuxedo, too.

But there was a drastic difference in them.

While at the wedding uncertainty shadowed Heather's eyes and doubt lurked in Kade's, only happiness shone in them now. Their postures were confident while Heather had hunched at her wedding. Kade had avoided looking at her then, and she was all he looked at now, their gazes so tender and their love so evident.

Mac couldn't be happier for his brother. While their start had been rocky, they'd gotten attached over the years, and his brotherly love had grown to the same level as with his blood-related brother.

Still, a bitter note tainted this sweetness, and he gulped his drink to chase away that bitterness. The beauty of the moment brought back his dreams as a teen.

Dreams of his wedding to Kimberly…

Enough!

He leaned toward his daughter, his wonderful treasure, and cut her food in small pieces. Her glass was empty now. "Would you like another drink?"

"Yes, Daddy."

The gaze of his daughter's eyes, the same shade as his own, never failed to soften him, soothe the pain just when it became sharp enough to slice him inside.

His brother wore his tuxedo like a second skin. On the contrary, Mac shifted in the chair, much preferring cowboy boots to polished shoes and a Wrangler shirt and jeans to a tuxedo.

But what wouldn't one do for his brother?

Liberty marched to him and dropped herself into the nearby chair draped in silk for the occasion, complete with the bow and a rose at the back.

It was a rare case of seeing her in a dress—especially a long spaghetti-strapped gown, a sacrifice to the image of the maid of honor—to the point that she could look like someone else. But the boots, the Stetson, emerald-green short hair, and that no-nonsense attitude on her makeup-free freckled face were soothingly familiar.

She gave his little girl a friendly hug and a doll, which earned her a squeal.

"Daddy, can I show it to Landon?" His daughter gestured to her toy.

He wanted to tell her to finish the food on her plate first, but he had a feeling Liberty wanted to talk to him alone.

He located his nephew with his gaze. "Sure, but not for long."

Liberty shifted close as soon as his daughter was gone.

"Are you okay?" she whispered, probably so the other guests wouldn't overhear.

As if not everyone in town had already known the story with Kimberly or the story with his ex. Part of small-town living, but he'd accepted it because it had a lot of perks, too.

Unlike Kimberly, he'd be lost in the big city.

For a no-nonsense tomboy, his sister had a sensitive side, too.

"Why wouldn't I be?" He shrugged nonchalantly.

"Oh, good." Her face relaxed. "I just thought… Never mind."

"You thought this reminded me of Kimberly, of that silly teenage idea to marry her someday." His gaze stayed focused on his girl, giggling and showing off her new prized possession to her cousin.

Kade looked at his glowing wife, a happy smile softening the hard lines of his face.

Their other brother, Maverick, had arrived for the occasion, taking a break from races—Maverick could afford it after he'd won several of the last ones—and had been talking to his childhood friend. Liberty, while unattached and scarred in her twenties, seemed happy enough. Their ranch, again, was doing great.

His gaze moved back to his daughter, and a warm tenderness spread inside him.

He had so much to be grateful to God for.

The present.

That was what he needed to focus on, not letting himself waver to the thoughts about Kimberly, his past.

By now, distant past.

"I did think about Kimberly." Liberty nodded as she studied him. Her voice dipped so low he had to strain to hear it. "What would you do if she returned? Would you give her another chance?"

Would he?

A pause stretched as his heart started beating faster and memories flooded in. "It's time for me to say a toast." He wasn't as eloquent as Kade, so he wasn't looking forward to it.

Liberty rolled her eyes. "Go ahead, avoid answering my question."

"I don't know," he offered the best he could.

"Don't worry. I'll say the toast as soon as I get to my seat." She rose. "Well, I sure hope she won't return because I might be tempted to punch her."

His sister—even if they weren't blood-related, he still always considered her his sister—marched back to her seat, stepped on her hem, and muttered something unflattering to the outfit.

For a moment, she eyed the knife, and he feared she'd cut the hem. Instead, she lifted her gown a little and marched further, probably promising herself never to wear the dress again.

"Daddy, I'm back!" His girl ran into his arms, and he gave her a gentle hug, love expanding his chest.

He told himself that was all he needed. But once disturbed, memories about Kimberly resurfaced, making his pulse erratic again.

Yes, it was a good thing she was never going to return, for more reasons than one.

Because he did know the answer, after all.

Despite everything she'd done.

Despite knowing she'd never stay in his hometown.

Despite him spending all these years doing his best to forget her.

Despite it all, he might be stupid enough to do everything he could to rekindle their love, at the risk of having his heart broken again.

THE END

THANK YOU FOR READING

Thank you for reading *Show Me a Marriage of Convenience*. If you write even several words on Amazon, BookBub, and/or Goodreads, it'll mean a lot to me. You can make a difference! I'm grateful to every person who reads my books, and every review matters to me.

What do you think about the series about single father cowboys and curvy heroines? This series has been so much fun to write! If you'd like to read Kimberly and Mac's story, it's Book 2, *Show Me a Second Chance.*

I do love hearing from readers, and if you email me at alexaverde7@gmail.com, or visit me on Goodreads, Facebook, BookBub, or Twitter, you'll make my heart sing. And if you'd like to know about my upcoming releases, please follow me on Amazon. Of course, I'd be thrilled if you looked at my other books, and I pray and hope they'll bring you joy and encouragement.

For giveaways, news, free ebooks, and recipes, please sign up for my newsletter. Subscribers have access to exclusive subscriber-only contests, subscriber free ebooks, and book news. Emails won't arrive more than weekly; your email address will never be passed on to anyone else, and you can unsubscribe at any time. Also, you'll get the download link for a FREE sweet Christian romance ebook, *Season of Mercy*, as soon as you confirm your email address as a thank you gift.

Thank you very much for sharing your time with me and my books, and I hope we'll meet again. God bless you.

With love,

Alexa Verde

ABOUT ALEXA VERDE

ALEXA VERDE writes sweet, wholesome books about faith, love, and murder. She has had 200 short stories, articles, and poems published in the five languages that she speaks. She has bachelor's degrees in English and Spanish, a master's in Russian, and enjoys writing about characters with diverse cultures. She's worn the hats of reporter, teacher, translator, model (even one day counts!), caretaker, and secretary, but thinks that the writer's hat suits her the best.

After traveling the world and living in both hemispheres, she calls a small town in south Texas home. The latter is an inspiration for the fictional setting of her series *Rios Azules Christmas* and *Secrets of Rios Azules.*

Please visit Alexa's website for more of her books and to sign up for her email newsletter: www.alexaverde.com

You can also find Alexa on social media:
Facebook : alexaverdeauthor
Twitter : alexaverde3
Goodreads : 8180452.Alexa_Verde
Bookbub : authors/alexa-verde
Amazon : amazon.com/author/alexaverde

BOOKS BY ALEXA VERDE

Christian Contemporary Romance

COWBOY CROSSING

Show Me A Marriage of Convenience (Book 1) (Kade and Heather

Show Me A Second Chance (Book 2) (Mac and Kimberly)

Show Me The Boss (Book 3) (Liberty and Kansas)

Show Me Best Friends (Book 4) (Maverick and Vera)

RIOS AZULES CHRISTMAS SERIES

In Love by Christmas Box Set (Season of Miracles, Season of Joy, Season of Hope)

Season of Miracles (*Book 1*) (Arturo and Lana)

Season of Joy (*Book 2*) (Dylan and Joy)

Season of Hope (*Book 3*) (Brandon and Kelly)

Christmas Love & Joy Box Set (Season of Love, Season of Miracles, Season of Joy)

RIOS AZULES ROMANCES: THE MACALISTERS SERIES

Season of Romance (*Book 1*) (Andrey and Melinda)

Season of Love (*Book 2*) (Petr and Lacy-Jane)

Season of Amor (*Book 3*) (Ray and Sylvia)

CHAPEL COVE ROMANCES SERIES

Love Me

Hold Me

Belong with Me

Christian Multicultural Romantic Suspense
Sweet, wholesome books about faith, love, and murder

SECRETS OF RIOS AZULES SERIES
Welcome to Rios Azules, a small south Texas town, where rivers and emotions run deep and the secrets are deadly.

Dangerous Love Box Set (Color of Danger, Taste of Danger, Touch of Danger)

River of Danger (*Prequel*) (Jacob and River)

Color of Danger (*Book 1*) (Luke and Mari)

Taste of Danger (*Book 2)* (James and Soledad)

Touch of Danger (*Book 3*) (Ivan and Julia)

Scent of Danger (*Book 4*) (Connor and Maya)

ACKNOWLEDGMENTS

Special thanks go to:

First of all, thank You to God for putting up with me and for all the blessings!

A millions thanks to you, my readers, for reading my books, for sending me encouragement, and for supporting me.

Heartfelt thanks to author Jessie Gussman for coming up with the idea for this series and for helping me so much on the way. Jessie, you make me laugh, you make me smile, and you make the world a better place.

Many thanks to my street team, Alexa's Amazing Readers, and to my beta readers, whom I love to pieces. Kim, Trudy, Paula, Susan, Jean, Deanna, Sarah, and Andrea, you're all amazing. Thank you, Renate and Edwina, for helping me to name several characters in this book. Thanks to Robin and Lisa for helping me name the horses.

I thank you wonderful editor, Deirdre, for coming through for me every time.

Last but in no way the least, thank you, Autumn. You're the best part of me.

Made in the USA
Monee, IL
15 July 2021

73681624R00132